PAT HUTCHINS

The House That Sailed Away

Illustrated by Laurence Hutchins

GREENWILLOW BOOKS
A Division of William Morrow & Company, Inc.
New York

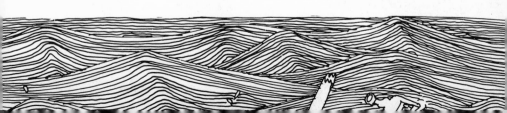

Printed in the United States of America.

1 2 3 4 5 / 79 78 77 76 75

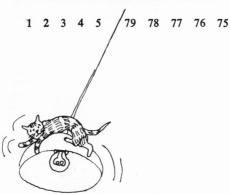

Library of Congress Cataloging in Publication Data
Hutchins, Pat, (date)   The house that sailed away.
SUMMARY: In a heavy rain Morgan's house floats from
London to the South Pacific where he and his family
confront cannibals and pirates.
[1. Humorous stories.   2. Fantasy]   I. Hutchins, Laur-
ence.   II. Title.
PZ7.H96165Ho   [Fic]   74-9823   ISBN 0-688-80013-0
ISBN 0-688-84013-2 lib. bdg.

This is
Morgan's story —
and Grandma's too.

Contents

1 The House That Sailed Away

It had rained every day since Grandma arrived in London. Every single day. Not the nice fat sort of rain that makes gentle plopping noises on your rainhat, or umbrella if you happened to have one, which Grandma hadn't as she'd left it on the overnight bus from Yorkshire, but the nasty thin sort of rain that runs down your nose and the tops of your Wellington boots and makes your hair stick out all over the place, especially if it's curly, which Grandma's was.

In fact it was the sort of weather you wouldn't turn a dog out in, if you liked dogs that is, which Grandma didn't anyway.

Grandma sighed deeply as she gazed out of the window. "Just think," she said gloomily, "if I hadn't done my ankle in at the Over 60's do, I would be visiting strange new places on the Cook's Coach and Paddle

1

Boat Mystery Tour, instead of sitting here staring at this awful rain."

She handed a curler to Mother, who was trying to set Grandma's hair, which Father said stuck up like steel wool after Mother had cleaned the inside of the oven with it.

"And if daft Betty from the shop hadn't shoved half a box of soap flakes all over the dance floor, I wouldn't have slipped in the first place."

"Or if she'd kept you off the vicar's home-made wine," Father murmured.

Grandma ignored him.

"I mean to say, I know the floor should have a nice slip to it, but she wouldn't listen when I told her you don't heap soap flakes on like it was French chalk." She shook her head and sighed again. "Mind you, if she'd ordered another packet of French chalk in the first place, like I told her to, she wouldn't have had to use the soap flakes. 'It'll give it a good slip,' she said. Aye, I'll say it gave it a good slip! When Elsie Bruce knocked Bob Bruce's pint of ale out of his hand during the conga, there was soapsuds everywhere. We all went down like ninepins; and as I'd just been up to collect my raffle prize, I was right at the end! Well, you can imagine. Bob Bruce is no lightweight, and Elsie's put on a fair bit of weight since you saw her last, and then there was fat Ginger and daft Betty." She paused for breath. "Eeh! It's a wonder I wasn't killed."

Father grinned and opened his mouth to speak, but Mother frowned at him and he shut it again.

"And to think," she added bitterly, "after I'd won two tickets for the mystery tour. Fancy having to give them away, and when my friend Kitty had arranged two weeks off to come with me as well."

"I thought you'd swapped them," said Father.

"Ah, but it's not the same, is it?" said Grandma. "Swapping first for second. Still, I couldn't very well go on a mystery tour with my ankle all done up in plaster, so I let Elsie and Bob Bruce have my tickets, and they insisted I have their prize instead."

"What was the second prize, Grandma?" asked Morgan, who was sitting at the window watching the rain.

"Two bottles," said Grandma.

"Aha!" Father winked at Morgan.

"But I gave one of them back for them to take in case the journey upset their stomachs. Tonic wine," she explained to Mother, who had finished setting Grandma's hair and was trying to rescue Tailcat from the baby, who had the cat's head stuck firmly under his arm while he tried to bite the threshing tail as it thumped backward and forward past his face.

Grandma suddenly sat bolt upright in her chair. "Eeh! it's funny you know," she said, "talking of upset stomachs, mine feels very peculiar." She patted her

4

stomach. "Just like it did the time I took our Dennis on a fishing boat in Whitby on his tenth birthday." She patted her stomach again. "Real weazy-like."

"I'll get your bottle of tonic wine," said Morgan, disappearing downstairs into the kitchen.

"Very peculiar," said Grandma, shaking her head.

"Very," Father agreed.

"Nine!" shouted Mother.

"What!" said Father, jumping up nervously.

"Nine!" Mother repeated.

"Nine what?" asked Grandma.

"Nine years old," said Mother.

"Nine years old, what?" demanded Father.

"Dennis was," said Mother. "He wasn't ten, he was nine. And it wasn't him anyway, it was me."

Father took a deep breath.

"All right," he said slowly. "It was you where?"

"On the fishing boat in Whitby, of course," said Mother brightly.

"Oh," said Father wearily, putting his earphones on to listen to a record.

"How strange," murmured Mother, looking down at the baby, who had started sliding slowly from one side of the room to the other. "I know this will sound silly, but the house seems to be—" she paused and picked up the baby as he slid by—"rocking," she finished.

At that moment Morgan burst into the room.

"Dad! Dad!" he shouted. "Quick! Downstairs! It's fantastic!"

"What?" said Father, who couldn't really hear as he was listening to a record of steam trains leaving King's Cross Station.

"The water!" yelled Morgan, so loudly he frightened Tailcat, who shot up in the air and started leaping around the room with his ears flat against his head and his fur standing on end.

"What on earth is happening?" said Father, as Tailcat landed on his shoulders, knocking his earphones off.

"Downstairs!" shouted Morgan, hopping from one foot to the other. "The water! Come and see!"

"What water where?" said Mother, trying to get up

from her chair, but the house seemed to be swaying so violently she sat down again. Grandma was clinging tightly to the sides of her armchair, looking very peaky.

Father jumped up quickly and ran downstairs after Morgan.

"Well!" said Mother, hanging on to Grandma's chair, which had started moving across the floor, with one hand and to the baby, who was trying to grab Tailcat every time he leaped past, with the other. "He might have told us what water was where, and why."

Suddenly there was a tremendous cracking noise and Grandma's chair slipped out of Mother's grip and rolled toward the window, where it stuck, pinning Grandma against the settee.

"Good heavens!" shrieked Grandma, as she looked

out of the window. The house shuddered and Grandma's chair rolled back again.

"I don't believe it," whispered Grandma faintly, as she slid past Mother's chair.

"Don't believe what?" asked Mother, clinging to the table and trying to free Tailcat from the baby, who was wrestling with him.

"We're only floating down Willow Road," snapped Grandma. "That's all!"

"Oh dear," said Mother, "what will the neighbors think?"

"I wish I'd stayed in Yorkshire," said Grandma, as the house lurched again, sending her chair rattling back across the room.

"It's incredible!" shouted Father, bursting into the room. "We're actually moving—the water is over the basement windows and nearly at the front door." He rushed over to the window. "Come and have a look!"

Morgan ran behind him. "There's Miss Johnson!" he shouted. "She looks a bit surprised!" He waved out of the window.

"I'd look surprised too," snapped Grandma, "if my next-door neighbor's house sailed away, taking my end wall with it!"

"Oh dear," said Mother, "poor Miss Johnson, it must be a bit drafty for her, especially with all this rain."

"Poor Miss Johnson," snorted Grandma. "What about me? I come down to London because I couldn't go on the mystery tour, thinking I'd have a nice quiet week to rest up my ankle, and what happens? I leave my umbrella on the bus, it rains every single day, spoiling my hairdo which I had done especially, and to top it all the house floats away, upsetting my stomach. And I never did get the wine I was promised," she added.

"I'm sorry, Grandma," said Morgan excitedly. "I forgot. I'll go and get it now. It's smashing in the kitchen with the water slapping at the window and all the plants floating about in it!"

"My plants!" wailed Mother, handing the baby to Grandma and rushing to the window.

"Isn't it fantastic?" said Father, opening the window so Mother could see better.

Mother couldn't believe her eyes.

The neighbors across the road were hanging out of their bedroom windows, waving and shouting, and on the smaller houses a bit farther down the hill the water was halfway up the front door, and people were climbing onto the roofs holding umbrellas and newspapers over their heads and staring in astonishment at them.

The Brown children were hanging out of their attic window, shouting and cheering and reaching out to try and touch the walls of the house as it slid slowly by them. Young Joseph started to cry and tried to clamber onto the roof, saying he wanted to go with Morgan, but his mother dragged him back in again.

Miss Johnson looked as if she'd turned to stone as she gazed at them through her lace curtains, with the rain beating against her as it blew in where the wall used to be. The few people who had been walking their dogs on the Heath were perched on the top branches of trees, looking very forlorn, with their dogs beside them.

All the cars that had been parked on Willow Road were floating around the house like pilot fish and Father was pleased he'd taken the Range Rover into the garage to have the windshield wipers fixed.

"My poor plants," said Mother sadly, as she saw her favorite geranium bobbing up and down in the water. "Still," she added, brightening up a bit, "at least they'll have plenty of water while we're away!"

Grandma cheered up quite a lot too after her glass of tonic wine and brought the baby to have a look out of the window, while Morgan went upstairs to the bedroom for a better view. Even Tailcat had calmed down and jumped onto the window ledge to have a sniff around, but changed his mind when he saw the baby and decided to curl up in Grandma's chair and go to sleep instead.

The house nearly stuck as it turned the corner at Willoughby Road, but Father and Morgan managed to push against the wall of the corner house with a broom and mop until it was free, and off they sailed into Hampstead High Street. The High Street was cluttered

with boxes of food that had floated out of the super-
market and bobbed against the open window of the
house, until Grandma decided they ought to take extra
provisions with them and leaned out and fished them
in, right in front of the police station too, although the
policemen were much too busy clinging to the roof and
trying to keep dry to care.

Soon they were gathering speed and the houses with the people on the roofs sped by as they sailed down the hill toward Camden Town.

"Isn't this exhilarating?" shouted Father, hanging out of the window.

"Well," said Mother uncertainly, "I suppose we always did want a sailing holiday, but I don't know what Morgan's teacher will say on Monday when he's not at school."

"Hooray!" shouted Morgan, who had heard her from the bedroom window. "No more school!"

"And Mother is getting her mystery tour after all," she added, "so that's not so bad, but there's one thing bothering me."

"What's that, dear?" asked Father, really enjoying himself now, as the house slipped into Camden Lock and floated along into Regent's Park Canal.

"We forgot to cancel the milk," said Mother.

"Ah well," said Grandma cheerfully, pouring herself another glass of wine, "worse things happen at sea."

A thick mist was forming as they drifted past the

zoo and Paddington Basin. By the time they had reached Brentford the fog was so dense it was impossible to see anything at all.

"I hope they don't," sighed Mother.

"Don't what?" said Father.

"Happen," said Mother.

Father closed his eyes for a moment. "You hope what won't happen?"

"Worse things," said Mother.

"Where?" said Father slowly.

"At sea, of course," said Mother.

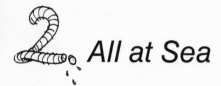 *All at Sea*

As it was beginning to get dark, Mother went to put the baby to bed, while Morgan and Father carried downstairs the boxes of food Grandma had retrieved from the water.

Grandma refused to go with them at first—she didn't like the thought of being underwater with all those fishes staring at her through the window—but eventually Morgan persuaded her, saying the fishes would be more scared of her, and Father said anything would be more scared of Grandma in her curlers.

So she crept downstairs after them, looking suspiciously at a pike that was banging its head against the glass in the kitchen door.

"It's very dark down here," Grandma complained, pressing the light switch. "Here," she added, as the light didn't come on, "it's not working!"

"Of course it's not working," said Father happily, getting the oil stove out of his work cupboard. "No lights, no cooker, no fridge, and no television."

"No television!" said Grandma in horror. "No telly!" she repeated, watching Father light the stove and put the kettle on. "And it's my favorite program tonight. 'Saturday Night at the London Palladium.' I never miss it. Never." She shook her head vigorously. "And it was Frankie Vaughan tonight. He's got such a lovely voice has Frankie, especially when he sings 'A rose I give to you.'" Grandma started singing softly to herself while Morgan unpacked the food, and Father said he'd just

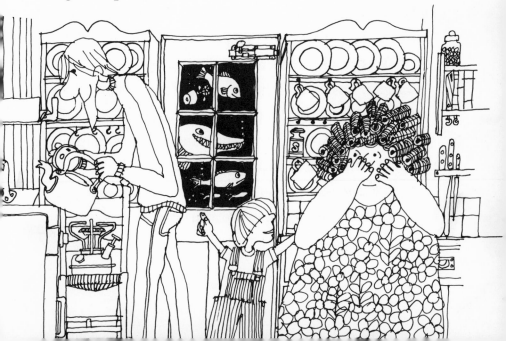

remembered something he'd forgotten to do upstairs.

They were very lucky really, the boxes were full of tins. Tins of meat, vegetables, milk, and fruit. So it didn't matter too much that the refrigerator wasn't working. Morgan stacked them in the cupboard, and Father came in with his model steam engines just as the kettle was boiling.

Grandma stopped singing and looked at him sharply, as he put the engines on the table, filled the boilers with boiling water, and lit the methylated spirit in the fuel box.

"Here we are," she said, "sitting in the dark, with no telly, drifting helplessly in the middle of the Atlantic Ocean, and you decide to play with your toys."

"Toys!" said Father in a shocked voice, turning to Morgan, who was helping him oil the wheels. "We're not playing with toys! We're conducting a scientific experiment. And besides," he added, gently patting an engine, "these aren't toys, they're models."

"It looks like playing to me," said Grandma.

"Steam," said Father, ignoring her remark, "so simple yet so versatile, a source of power and of light."

"I don't see any light," Grandma interrupted.

"We haven't finished yet," said Father calmly.

"Oh," said Grandma in a sarcastic sort of voice, "then while you're finishing your scientific experiment, I'll look for the candles." And she started rummaging through the drawers in the sideboard.

"You won't find any in there," said Father, after Grandma had emptied every drawer.

"Mummy keeps the candles in the vegetable rack," said Morgan, "but I think there's only a Christmas candle left because she melted the others down to make wax animals for the school bazaar."

"Well, that's not going to last long," said Grandma, producing from the vegetable rack the stub of a candle decorated with angels and banging it down on the table.

"It's all right, Grandma," said Morgan, helping Father wire up the engines to small electric motors. "We've nearly finished."

Grandma started coughing as the engines spluttered and hissed and belched smoke from their chimneys.

"Just look at them," said Father in admiration, as he set them down gently on the carpet. "Look at all that pressure! All that energy! Remarkable!"

Grandma dabbed her eyes, which were watering, with the edge of the tablecloth.

"I don't see anything remarkable," she coughed, "in toys that sit on the floor, blowing whistles that scare you to death and smoke that chokes you to death."

"We're off!" shouted Father in excitement.

"We're off! We're off!" echoed Morgan, dancing in delight as the engines slowly lurched forward and then gradually picked up speed until they were clattering around the room so fast it made Grandma dizzy to look at them.

The noise was deafening as Mother felt her way down the darkened stairs into the kitchen, followed by Tailcat, who had woken up.

"Good heavens!" she gasped, as she opened the door.

Through the haze of thick black smoke Mother saw Grandma, sitting on the kitchen table with a wet dish-

cloth covering her face and a tea towel wrapped round her ears, fanning herself with yesterday's newspaper.

Father and Morgan were leaping around the room, waving a can of oil and laughing, while on the kitchen sink two tiny little light bulbs flickered on and off as the engines thundered round and round the smoke-filled room.

Tailcat ran back upstairs as Mother rushed to the window, completely forgetting they were under water and not even noticing the shoals of tiny luminous fish, glittering in the darkness outside.

"What we need," she said, heaving at the sash window, "is some fresh air in here."

"Don't do that!" yelled Father and Morgan, trying to scramble to the window but tripping over the engines as they steamed between their feet.

"Oh dear!" said Mother, as the window opened and the water poured in, bouncing off the chaise longue and slowly filling the room, until it crept up over the engines, which spluttered to a standstill with a sharp hiss of steam.

The room was quite dark, apart from the light from the stove, as Father and Morgan splashed across to the window and forced it down again.

"Oh dear," Mother repeated, as a fish swam past, tickling her ankle.

"What's going on? What's going on?" shouted Grandma from the tabletop.

"Mother forgot," said Father wearily, lighting a match and looking at the damage.

"And now we can't see," said Morgan. "The steam engines won't work and we haven't any candles."

"Yes we have!" said Mother, cheering up a bit. "I bought a few boxes for Grandma's birthday, don't you remember? We were going to put them on a cake, but Father said we'd never make a cake big enough to take them all, so they're still in the fridge."

"Birthday candles," said Father, "in the fridge." He closed his eyes.

"Beggars can't be choosers," snapped Grandma through the darkness.

"Well," he added briskly, "if they were for Grandma's birthday cake, there's bound to be quite a lot of them, so birthday candles or not, they'll have to do. We've got to bale this water out tonight." He turned to Mother. "Through the upstairs window, dear," he said gently, "please."

That first night at sea was spent carrying buckets of water up the stairs by the light of dozens of flickering pink and blue candles, and when the last drop of water had been mopped up from the floor and the steam engines carefully wiped and oiled and put away, Mother smiled gently to herself. "Doesn't it look lovely?" she said, looking at the candles and the multicolored fish that darted up to the window, glittering in the inky black sea.

"Just like Christmas," she added.

"Let's go to bed," said Father wearily.

And as the house gently bobbed across the ocean, they all slept remarkably well, considering.

3 Worse Things Do Happen at Sea

The next few weeks were quite busy. With no electricity the housework took much longer to do. Mother and Grandma had to clean the stairs with a handbrush and the carpets with a sweeper as they couldn't use the vacuum cleaner.

All the cooking, of course, had to be done on the oil stove, and they boiled sea water to do the dishes. Father had looked in the water tank and noticed it was only half full and said they must reserve fresh water as much as possible, and as it was getting warmer, they could bathe in the sea.

Grandma didn't like that idea very much, as she hadn't brought a swimming suit with her and Mother's were much too small for her; but eventually Mother persuaded her to wrap a towel round herself instead, and after Grandma had insisted Father stayed in the

basement and didn't peep, Morgan tied a length of rope round Grandma's waist (she couldn't swim very well) and held the end as she lowered herself through the window and into the water, clinging to the window sill with one hand, while she soaped herself with the other.

Father soon had the steam engines working again, and on Mother's insistence, clamped them to the kitchen table. The motors still worked and produced a little light, but it wasn't such good fun. They found that by opening the doors on the stairs and the windows in the living room above, the smoke cleared away quite well. Father and Morgan had tied a couple of kitchen chairs onto the roof, and with Father's binoculars strapped to the television aerial, the chairs made quite a good lookout, or crow's-nest, as Father insisted on calling it, which they got to by climbing through the skylight in the attic. Grandma refused to go and look, on account of her ankle, and said anyway there was only sea to look at when she got there, and she'd seen enough of that already. So she held the baby, while Mother climbed up the ladder onto the roof.

It was a lovely warm afternoon. The sky was a brilliant blue, and the sea sparkled and glittered in the sunlight.

"Oh look!" said Mother, squinting through the binoculars. "I can see a ship!"

"What?" said Father, trying to peer over her shoulder.

"I can see a ship," Mother repeated, "and I know this may sound silly," she added, "but it looks like a . . ." she peeped through the binoculars again, "pirate ship to me."

"Don't be so silly, dear," said Father impatiently, "there aren't any pirates nowadays."

Mother sat down on one of the chairs.

"All right then," she said, "you have a look!"

Father bent down toward the binoculars.

"Good heavens!" he shouted. "You're absolutely right!"

"What is it? What is it?" said Morgan, scrambling up the ladder with Tailcat, whom he'd rescued from the baby, under his arm.

"Pirates!" said Mother proudly.

"Yikes!" whispered Morgan, hopping up and down and trying to get to the binoculars that Father was still bent over. "Real live pirates? Flying the Skull and Crossbones? Wait till I tell them at school!"

"What's going on up there?" Grandma's face peered up at them through the skylight.

"It's all right, Grandma," said Mother. "Father thought I was seeing things, but I wasn't, because when he looked he saw them too."

"Oh!" said Grandma. "Here!" She looked up suspiciously. "What sort of things?"

"Pirates!" shouted Morgan, as Father moved to let

him have a look through the binoculars. "Hundreds of them! With big cutlasses and black patches over their eyes!"

Grandma shuddered and clutched the baby tightly.

"Eeh! Stop it, our Morgan, you've made me come out goosy all over."

"It's true! It's true!" cried Morgan excitedly. "Come and see!"

"You're not getting me up that ladder," said Grandma, "pirates or no pirates!"

"They don't look too friendly either," said Father, "and they seem to be heading this way."

"I hope they're not planning a visit," said Mother anxiously, "because there seems to be an awful lot of them and I don't think we have enough teacups to go round." She looked thoughtfully out to sea. "Of course we could always offer them a glass of rum."

"I shouldn't start giving them rum," Grandma called. "You know what these pirates are like with their yo-ho-hoy."

"I hadn't thought of that," admitted Mother.

"Well, we'd better start thinking now," said Father, pointing toward the pirate ship. They could just see it now without using the binoculars.

Morgan looked disappointed as the ship got nearer. "It looks more like a paddle steamer than a pirate ship to me," he said. But he did like the lovely big Skull and Crossbones they were flying.

"Good heavens!" exclaimed Father, peering through

the binoculars again. *"Heart of Hull*—what a strange name for a pirate ship!"

"Hull!" shrieked Grandma, suddenly dropping into a chair in the bedroom. "Hull's in Yorkshire! Here," she added, "what name did you say it was?"

"Heart of Hull," Father shouted down.

"Oh my goodness!" said Grandma faintly, clutching her forehead. Morgan looked down the skylight at her.

"What's wrong?" he asked anxiously. "Shall I get you a glass of tonic wine?"

"Oh yes, please!" said Grandma quickly. "I seem to have taken quite a turn." She took a deep breath. *"Heart of Hull,"* she said dramatically, "was the paddle steamer on the Cook's Mystery Tour!"

"What?" said Father.

"Are you sure?" asked Mother.

"Yes," said Grandma, "it said so on the tickets. 'The tour will depart from Richmond bus station at 15.00 hours, and connect with the paddle steamer *Heart of Hull* at 17.00 hours which will make many interesting ports of call.' "

31

"Oh dear," said Mother, "how dreadful! Poor Mr. and Mrs. Bruce!"

"Do you think they were made to walk the plank?" whispered Morgan, who had returned with the wine and was listening open-mouthed to Grandma. "Or thrown to the sharks?"

"Don't say that, our Morgan," said Grandma nervously, gulping wine down and refilling her glass. "It makes my legs go all wobbly."

"We're not scared of pirates, are we, Daddy?" shouted Morgan. "We'll punch them and bite their noses and pull their beards and biff them and bash them all over the place! Won't we?"

"Now then, dear," said Mother, "don't get excited, they might not be as bad as all that. They might even be nice pirates who like little boys."

"They don't look it," said Morgan gleefully, pointing to the paddle steamer.

The steamer had dropped anchor and a bunch of wild-looking pirates were leaping into a rowboat, waving their cutlasses in the direction of the house.

"Well," said Mother, "I'd better take the baby for his afternoon nap—not that he'll get much sleep with that racket going on," she added, as bloodcurdling yells pierced the air.

"Aha!" said Father, who had been thoughtfully stroking his chin. "I have a plan! Come on, Morgan," he added briskly, "we've work to do."

So while Mother put the baby to bed, and Grandma went down to the kitchen to look for the heaviest pan she could find, just in case, Father and Morgan worked out their plan.

When Mother got back, she was rather surprised to see that Morgan and Father had dismantled the clothes line from the kitchen; and hanging from the roof through the attic was a strange contraption of ropes and wheels, attached to the end of which and dangling a few inches above the bedroom floor was the log basket. Mother and Father's bed had been pushed against the wall, and in its place was a pile of logs that they'd got in especially for Christmas and had kept stored in the back of Father's work cupboard. Mother could hear Father and Morgan rushing about on the roof and the shouts of the pirates as their rowboat moved swiftly across the water toward the house.

"Quick!" cried Father, leaning through the skylight. "Fill the basket!"

"They're attacking! They're attacking!" sang Morgan. Mother couldn't hear, what with the pirates yelling and Morgan shouting and Grandma rattling pans in the kitchen.

"What did you say, dear?" she asked.

"Fill the basket!" roared Father, stabbing his finger toward the pile of logs.

"What for?" asked Mother curiously.

Father closed his eyes. "So we can sink their boat!" he shouted.

"What a good idea," she said.

So Mother filled the basket, and as Father quickly pulled it up, an impatient Morgan hopped from one foot to the other, waiting for his armful of ammunition to drop on the howling pirates, who had reached the house and were tying their rowboat to the brass handle on the front door.

Grandma was just on her way up from the kitchen, clutching a heavy iron frying pan, when an evil face, with a patch over one eye and a dagger between its teeth, leered at her through the living room window. It was One-Eyed Jake, the notorious boss of a gang of hooligans that police all over the world had been trying to catch, climbing up the drainpipe.

Grandma screamed and ran upstairs to the bedroom, as his hairy legs disappeared up the wall.

"Hello," said Mother, as Grandma burst into the room. "I'm glad your ankle seems to be getting better."

One-Eyed Jake was heaving himself up to the sill to

35

have a look in, when the bedroom window flew open, and an iron pan came crashing down on the top of his head and the window shut again with a bang.

"That'll teach him," said Grandma indignantly.

All One-Eyed Jake saw was stars, as he crashed backward into the sea, knocking his mates, who were climbing up after him, into the water with him. Morgan and Father laughed and ran to and fro with armloads of logs and dropped them from the roof, so that they bounced off the heads of the pirates and crashed onto the rowboat, which slowly sank under the sea; leaving Jake and his cronies thrashing about in the water, howling and cursing, as they swam back to the paddle steamer.

They watched until the pirates had scrambled aboard the paddle steamer, and their shouting and cursing melted into the sound of the sea as the paddle steamer turned round and disappeared over the horizon.

"What shocking language!" said Grandma angrily, waving the frying pan at the retreating vessel.

"We shown 'em, we shown 'em, didn't we, Dad!" shouted Morgan, his face flushed with victory.

"I have a feeling," said Father slowly, "that we haven't seen the last of that gang of cutthroats."

"Showed," said Mother.

"What?" said Father.

"Showed," Mother repeated.

"Showed what?" sighed Father.

"The pirates, of course," said Mother brightly. "We didn't shown 'em, we showed them."

"Oh," said Grandma, Father, and Morgan.

4. The Message

They didn't in fact see any sign of the pirates during the next few days, although they all took turns at the lookout, except for Grandma, who had decided to stay in bed to recover from the shock and read the story she'd started on the bus but hadn't had time to finish.

The baby had started crawling, which meant he could chase Tailcat around the house, which was very nice for him but not so nice for Tailcat as the baby had just cut his two front teeth.

Father and Morgan invented all kinds of useful gadgets, which Mother couldn't work out how to use, and everyone was turning a lovely golden brown as the sun streaming through the top floor windows got hotter every day.

"You know," said Mother, as they all sat down to breakfast one morning, "I'm really quite enjoying this trip. It's a pity that we haven't any food left."

"What!" said Father, Morgan, and Grandma.

"I said I'm really quite enjoying this trip," Mother repeated, opening a tin of custard. "Apart from the pirates, of course," she added, "although they didn't really seem to be so bad." She looked thoughtfully at the custard. "There again they might have been, I suppose, depending on whether they made poor Mr. and Mrs. Bruce walk the plank or not."

"Did you say," said Father slowly, "that there isn't any food left?"

"Oh, it's all right, dear," said Mother gaily, "there's this tin of custard for breakfast."

"A tin of custard," sighed Father, "for breakfast."

"I don't like tinned custard," said Grandma.

"What about lunch?" asked Morgan.

"I hadn't thought of that," Mother admitted.

"Come on, Morgan," said Father, getting up from the table, "we've work to do."

The baby ate the whole tin of custard, as no one else seemed to want any, while Father and Morgan rigged up two fishing rods from a bamboo cane, some empty spools of thread, twine from Morgan's kite, and two of the baby's diaper pins.

"Don't go catching any of those nasty lobster things," said Grandma, shuddering. "I can't stand them. Marching about sideways as if they owned the place, with all those horrible hairy arms pinching about. It's not as though they even taste nice," she added indignantly.

After the baby had finished his breakfast, Mother carried him upstairs to have a crawl around on the living room floor.

"Eeh!" said Grandma, struggling up the stairs after them and nearly tripping over Tailcat who had heard the baby coming up and was on his way down. "My stomach is beginning to feel right weazy again."

"It's probably the thought of the hairy arms," said Mother, setting the baby on the floor and watching Father, who had his sleeves rolled up, casting his line through the open window.

"They're not that bad," said Grandma in surprise, looking at Father's arms.

"Oh," said Mother absently, "I thought you couldn't stand them."

"Now, I never said that," said Grandma, getting flustered. "I might have said they were a bit on the skinny side, but I never said I couldn't stand them."

"How strange," murmured Mother, frowning to herself. "I must have imagined it, but you know, I was quite sure you said so at breakfast, because I was thinking how nice one would be, grilled in butter, then you said you didn't like the way they marched sideways."

"Aha!" shouted Grandma. "I know what you're talking about!"

"You do?" asked Mother, looking puzzled.

"Lobsters!" said Grandma triumphantly.

"What on earth is going on?" said Father in a muffled voice, as a sharp gust of wind caught the curtain and wrapped it round him.

"It's the wind," said Grandma in satisfaction, "blowing us about. That's what's upsetting my stomach."

"Oh dear," said Mother, as Morgan unwrapped Father, "it seems to be getting awfully dark."

"Yikes!" whispered Morgan. "Look at that!" He pointed through the window. A huge black mass of clouds had blotted out the sun and was slowly creeping across the blue sky.

"It looks as if we're in for a storm," said Father.

Grandma shrieked and leaped out of her chair as a brilliant sheet of lightning lit up the sky and a great crack of thunder shook and rolled around the house.

"Quick!" said Father, banging the window shut and trapping Morgan's fishing rod in it, as icy rain slashed against the glass. "The upstairs windows!"

Morgan and Father raced upstairs to the bedrooms, while Mother picked up the baby and Grandma staggered over to the drink cupboard to have a glass of tonic wine to settle her stomach.

Tailcat came flying upstairs to see what was going on, skidded on the rug, and ended up on Mother's knee with the baby, who gurgled happily, grabbed his head, and squeezed it under his arm, until Mother freed it, as Tailcat didn't seem to like it very much.

Grandma was having trouble trying to pour a glass

of wine and decided to drink from the bottle instead.

Mother thought it was safer to sit on the floor with the baby on her lap and hang onto the grate of the fireplace, which the baby liked, because he could just reach part way up the chimney, where nice little piles of soot had settled.

Grandma decided to sit on the floor too, and wedged herself firmly between the wall and the drink cupboard, with the bottle clasped between her knees. "If I'd known," said Grandma bitterly, "what I was letting myself in for when I booked my ticket for the overnight bus, I'd never have set foot in that booking office."

The house lurched violently, and Tailcat, who had escaped from the baby and was clinging to the armchair, leaped into the air and landed on the lampshade as it swung past him.

The baby liked that, and held his sooty arms up to try and grab the cat's tail every time he sailed past.

"What a fantastic storm!" shouted Father, as he and Morgan burst into the room. "It's a good thing we've got television!"

"Huh!" snorted Grandma scornfully, "a fat lot of good telly is when you can't watch it!"

"Lightning conductor!" Father shouted. "The aerial."

"Well then," said Grandma sarcastically, "in that case I suppose it's worth paying the B.B.C. twelve pounds a year for a color television license, just in case your house happens to float away and be battered by storms in the middle of the Atlantic Ocean."

"Pacific," Father corrected.

The house lurched again and the empty glass Grandma had taken out for her wine slipped off the drink cupboard and bounced down onto Grandma's head.

"Eeh!" said Grandma in alarm. "It's a good job I've got my curlers in." She patted the metal curlers. "I might have been killed!"

Father grinned and was about to say something, but Mother put her finger to her lips and shook her head.

"Oh look!" cried Morgan in excitement. "I think I've caught something!" He stumbled across to the window, opened it, and pulled the line in.

"The only thing we're likely to catch," Grandma complained, as the rain blew in and beat against her face, "is our death of cold!"

"Oh!" said Morgan in a disappointed voice, closing the window and holding up a bottle.

"Let me see that bottle, our Morgan," shouted Grandma from the corner.

"It's empty, Grandma," said Morgan.

"Oh," said Grandma.

"Oh no, it's not!" shouted Morgan, shaking the bottle. Grandma's face lit up.

"Look! There's a message in it," Morgan cried, staggering across to where Grandma was wedged, dodging the chairs as they rattled around the room.

Grandma's face fell again. "Oh," she said, "is that all? Here!" she added, grabbing the bottle.

"What is it?" Mother called anxiously, as Grandma clutched her forehead.

"Eeh! I think I'm having another turn," whispered Grandma faintly, taking a swig from her bottle.

"What's wrong?" asked Morgan in alarm.

"It's the sight of an empty bottle," laughed Father. Grandma ignored that remark.

"This bottle," she said, holding the bottle above her head, "is the same," she continued, "as this bottle." She held her own bottle up. "This bottle," she added dramatically, shaking the bottle with the message in it, "is the selfsame bottle I gave to the Bruces to take with them on the Mystery Tour!"

"Good heavens!" said Father.

"Are you sure?" asked Mother.

"Absolutely!" said Grandma, pointing to the side of the bottle where part of a label was still visible. "See that mark? That's where that daft Betty from the shop stamped second prize all over the label in indelible ink."

"Take the cork out! Take the cork out!" sang Morgan, jumping up and down and nearly losing his balance as the house lurched again and Tailcat fell from the lampshade and landed on his head.

"I'm trying to," puffed Grandma, heaving at the bottle, "but the house is rattling about so much I can't get a good grip."

Father and Morgan stumbled over to Grandma to help pull. They heaved and heaved until suddenly the cork popped out. Morgan and Father fell over, the house listed with an alarming scraping sound, and the bottle fell out of Grandma's grip and rolled down the sloping floor to where Mother and the baby were clinging to the grate.

"Good gracious!" exclaimed Mother, pulling the paper out of the bottle and reading it. "It says, 'Help! We're stranded on a desert island!'"

The house was very still, as Father picked himself up from the floor.

"And it looks," he said, pointing to the window, where a palm tree was pressed against the glass, "as if they're not the only ones!"

 # Stranded!

They certainly were stranded on a desert island. By the time they'd all rushed downstairs and Father had oiled the back door lock (it had rusted rather badly being under water for so long), the storm clouds had completely cleared and the sun was streaming in through the kitchen window.

"Oh," said Mother, clapping her hands in delight as the door creaked open, "isn't it lovely?"

"Just think," she said to Father and Morgan, who couldn't hear her as they'd already kicked off their shoes and were chasing each other round the beach.

"Just think," she repeated to Grandma, who was still standing there, looking a bit bewildered. "Only a few months ago we were sitting in Willow Road with all that dreadful rain, and now here we are—" she waved her hand toward the golden beach and the dark green clusters of palm trees—"washed up on a beautiful desert island, a thousand miles from anyone!" Mother paused, as she remembered the note in her hand. "Of course," she continued, "if the Bruces are marooned on this island, we probably won't be a thousand miles from anyone. Unless, of course, they're on the other side of the island, in which case we could still be a thousand miles from anyone."

"Oh!" said Grandma, looking at Mother in a funny way.

"Depending on the size of the island, of course," Mother finished.

Tailcat, who had been standing on the doorstep, sniffing, decided it was safe to walk on the beach and stepped gingerly onto the sand, while the baby struggled in Mother's arms to get down and chase him. So Mother got his stroller, while Grandma put her hat on and wrapped a woolly blanket around herself so she wouldn't get sunstroke. Then they stepped out onto the beach.

Grandma wobbled forward for a few steps, then fell

in a heap onto the sand, knocking her feathered hat all lopsided.

"Oh dear!" said Mother, trying to pull her up. "Are you all right?"

"No!" said Grandma crossly, pushing her hat back as Father and Morgan ran over to help. "This beach is worse than the Big Dipper at Blackpool."

Father laughed as they all heaved and managed to get Grandma on her feet again. "It's your sea legs!" he said. "You'll soon get used to it. Or the wine," he whispered to Morgan.

Grandma hung onto the handle of the stroller and they managed to steer her over to a clump of coconut trees, where she insisted on sitting, as it was nice and shady, with the blanket wrapped tightly round her so she wouldn't get burned and her hat wedged firmly over her curlers.

Father and Morgan were splashing about in the sea in front of the house, and Mother decided to let the baby have a little paddle, as the water was very warm. The baby liked having his toes dipped in the water and splashing Tailcat, who was hovering at the water's edge.

"What about the Bruces?" Mother shouted to Father and Morgan.

"Good heavens!" said Father, "I'd completely forgotten about them." He looked thoughtfully at the house. "Well, Morgan and I could always go and search for them, although it wouldn't exactly be a rescue. As we're marooned too."

"We could always send a message in Grandma's bottle," Mother suggested. "After all, their message was found." Mother frowned. "Although I don't suppose there are too many houses floating around this part of the world. Still," she added, brightening up, "there might be a boat pass by."

"Yes," said Father grimly, "and it might just be a pirate boat!"

They decided not to send a message for the moment, just in case, but that Father and Morgan should look for the Bruces, while Mother and Grandma collected pineapples and coconuts for lunch. Mother waved to Grandma, who was still huddled under the trees

wrapped in the blanket, and went into the house to collect her shopping basket. Father and Morgan filled a flask with water and collected a few bits and pieces from the work cupboard that might be useful in the search. Mother put the baby's sunhat on his head and went outside to call for Grandma. She saw the gray blanket lying under the trees, but no Grandma. Grandma had completely disappeared.

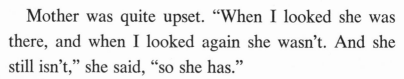

"Father!" Mother shouted. "Grandma's vanished."

"Don't be silly, dear," said Father, coming to the door. "Grandma never vanishes."

Mother was quite upset. "When I looked she was there, and when I looked again she wasn't. And she still isn't," she said, "so she has."

Father shielded his eyes against the sun and looked across to where Grandma had been sitting.

"Good heavens!" shouted Father in delight. "I do believe you're right!"

"What is it? What is it?" asked Morgan, running out of the house.

"Grandma's gone," wailed Mother.

"Where to?" asked Morgan.

"We don't know," said Father, patting Mother's shoulder, "but she can't have got far in those shoes she was wearing."

"Why don't we go and look through the binoculars?" Morgan suggested.

"What a good idea!" Mother exclaimed, cheering up a bit.

Morgan led the way into the house and up the stairs, followed by Mother, who had insisted on going too, and Father, who was struggling behind with the baby, who happened to be very fond of Father's nose and liked to try and twist it off, which was a little uncomfortable for Father, as it had got rather sunburned in the last few days.

They climbed up the ladder onto the roof and Father handed the baby back to Mother with relief, as Morgan bent over the binoculars to look for Grandma.

"Y-y-y-yikes!" stuttered Morgan, his face pink with excitement.

"What is it? What is it?" asked Mother, trying to peer over Morgan's shoulder.

"Good heavens!" said Father slowly, as Morgan stepped back, speechless with surprise, to let Father look.

"Let me see," said Mother nervously, as Father straightened up with a you-could-knock-me-over-with-a-feather sort of look on his face.

"Oh dear!" said Mother, clamping her hand over her mouth.

Through the binoculars she could see, quite clearly, a sand dune. And disappearing over the ridge were lots of tiny little men. And held high above their heads, with her legs waving wildly in the air, was a plump lady in a feathered hat.

"Grandma!" Mother gasped.

Cannibal Pots

Mother was in quite a state about it all, but Father managed to calm her down by saying he and Morgan would go and try to rescue Grandma, if the little men had decided to keep her, that is, which he doubted anyway.

He made Mother lock herself and the baby in the house, while he and Morgan set off.

It was quite easy to see which way they'd taken Grandma. All they had to do was follow the footprints in the sand, and there were lots of those. Grandma must have been quite a weight for the little men to carry because every few yards there were big dents in the sand where they'd obviously set her down to have a rest.

They followed the tracks across the island until in front of them they saw a clearing, surrounded by grass huts. The footprints led straight into it.

"Quick!" whispered Father to Morgan. "Behind here!"

They hid behind a banana tree, and peeped out, and through a gap between the huts they saw Grandma sitting on a wooden throne, looking remarkably cheery, as men, women, and children danced up to her with steaming dishes of food, smiling happily and pinching her plump arms as they set the dishes down before her.

Father whistled as he saw the little children rubbing their tummies every time they looked at her. "I suspect," said Father, "that Grandma may have been captured by cannibals."

"Are they going to eat her?" Morgan whispered, as the chief carried a big iron pot out of his hut.

"It certainly looks like it," Father admitted. He watched the children pile dried grass around the pot.

"I suppose we ought to try and do something—Mother will be awfully upset if they do."

"I expect Grandma will be too," said Morgan, peeping out to see if they'd put her in the pot yet. At that very moment Grandma turned round and spotted them.

"Yoo hoo!" she called, waving a dish of baked bananas above her head. "Come and meet my nice new friends. They seem to have invited me to lunch."

In no time at all they were surrounded and taken to the chief, who was fanning Grandma with palm leaves and offering her little coconut cakes smothered in honey from half a scooped-out pineapple.

"Come and sit down," said Grandma, patting the huge throne and hitching up a bit to make room. She smiled coyly at the chief, who was looking at Father's thin arms in a disappointed sort of way.

"Grandson!" she beamed proudly, patting Morgan's head. The chief grinned and rubbed his stomach.

"Son-in-law!" she added apologetically, jerking her head toward Father, who was sitting all hunched up looking miserable.

"Eeh!" Grandma went on breathlessly. "What a pity Mother and the baby didn't come. I'm having such a lovely time! They can't do enough for me. Insisted on carrying me here too, although I must admit, I struggled a bit at first." She giggled and blushed as she bent over to Morgan's ear. "But they're so strong," she whispered, "and don't you think the chief is ever so handsome? Just like Rudolph Valentino. Eeh!" She sighed happily. "My friend Kitty will be green with jealousy when I tell her."

She offered Morgan the dish of bananas. "Try these," she said, "they're delicious, they don't taste like foreign food at all. I've had six already. Still," she added, "I can always go on a diet tomorrow."

"No thank you," said Morgan, eying the fire under the pot, which was blazing now. "I don't feel hungry."

"Oh, you must eat something," said Grandma cheerfully, "or the chief will be terribly upset, especially after he's gone to so much trouble." She smiled shyly at the chief, who grinned back and pinched her on the cheek.

"Oh," giggled Grandma, slapping his hand playfully, "you are a one!"

Father stared gloomily at the fire. The water in the pot was beginning to bubble.

"Eeh," said Grandma, noticing the pot, "I hope they're not going to cook anything else. I'm fair fit to burst!"

Some of the men carried drums out of the huts and started beating them in front of the boiling pot. Grandma tapped her feet and hummed softly to herself as she swayed to the music.

"This takes me back," she murmured.

The chief bent down to her, his arms outstretched, smiling broadly. Grandma giggled and shook her head. "If you don't mind, I'll sit this one out." She patted her stomach. "Too full," she explained. But of course the chief didn't understand, and as he was still hovering, holding out his arms, Grandma decided it might seem rude to refuse, and taking his hand, stepped daintily into the clearing.

To Father and Morgan's astonishment and the chief's delight, Grandma suddenly went into a wild dance. Everyone clapped their hands and danced in a circle around Grandma, who was tossing the chief into the air (as he was much lighter than she) and twirling him round her head before catching him as he dropped down again.

The chief seemed to be really enjoying himself, until Grandma suddenly stopped to mop her face, which had got very hot and flushed. Then he looked at her in concern, pinched her cheek again, and waved to the drummers to stop playing. Then taking Grandma gently by the hand, he led her across to the boiling pot.

"Yikes!" whispered Morgan.

"Oh, oh!" said Father.

"No thank you," said Grandma sweetly, as the chief pointed inside the pot. "I really couldn't eat another thing."

The men who had carried Grandma to the village and had been lying down to recover scowled and staggered to their feet as the chief clicked his fingers toward them. They tottered over to Grandma, wobbling a bit, then heaved and heaved until eventually they managed to lift her off her feet. Just as they were about

to drop her into the boiling water, Father and Morgan jumped up, ran across the clearing, and dived at their legs. The men collapsed like ninepins as a giggling Grandma crashed down on top of them, pinning them to the ground and breaking her fall.

"Eeh!" Grandma laughed in delight, picking herself up and straightening her hat to cover up the curlers. "Aren't they cheeky little fellows?"

The chief was jumping up and down and shouting at the men lying on the ground, but they only shouted back when he pointed at Grandma, and crawled over to a hut where they lay muttering to themselves and trying to get their breath back.

"Here we go again," murmured Father as more men, armed with spears this time, crept warily across, eying Grandma suspiciously.

Father and Morgan were grabbed by four of them, leaving the other dozen or so to handle Grandma, who was lifted, struggling, over the pot again. Father closed his eyes, waiting for the splash, but Morgan couldn't resist a little peep.

"Dad!" he whispered, shaking Father's arm. "Look!"

Father opened one eye. Through Grandma's waving arms he saw two bedraggled figures wandering into the clearing. They stopped dead when they saw Grandma.

"Well, I never did," gasped one.

"You could knock me over with a feather," said the other.

"Lily Goundry!" they both shouted.

The little men set Grandma on the ground again when they heard the voices.

"Eeh!" said Grandma in disbelief, as she turned to look at the couple. "Eeh!" she repeated faintly. "Elsie and Bob Bruce! Fancy meeting you here!"

7. Long-Lost Friends

Father and Morgan could hardly believe their eyes, and Grandma had to sit down for a few minutes, she felt so funny. The Bruces, of course, were practically speechless, which was unusual for them, because Mrs.

Bruce especially liked a good gossip. The most surprising thing of all, though, was that the cannibals were absolutely delighted to see the Bruces, and the chief positively beamed when he saw them, and kept hugging and kissing them on both cheeks, as though welcoming long-lost friends.

"By gum," said Mr. Bruce slowly, when he'd got his tongue back. "Would you believe it, our Elsie?" he asked, turning to his wife.

"If someone had said to me," said Mrs. Bruce, "when we swapped prizes at the Over 60's do, that we would bump into Mrs. Goundry again in the middle of a desert island, I'd never have believed them. Never!" she repeated, shaking her head.

"It's a small world," Mr. Bruce admitted.

"Aye! It is that," Mrs. Bruce agreed.

"How," asked Father nervously, looking at the cannibals, who had set down their spears and were standing in little groups around the Bruces, chattering and laughing, "did you get to know the—" he cleared his throat and lowered his voice—"cannibals?" he whispered.

"Oh yes!" said Grandma, fluttering her eyelashes at the chief. "Do tell us how you got to know them." Grandma's voice trailed off and the brilliant smile she was flashing to the chief froze on her face. "Here!" she gasped, grabbing Father's arm. "What did you say?"

"Cannibals," Father hissed, which was difficult to do as he was smiling weakly at the chief at the same time. Grandma shrieked and clutched her forehead.

"Cannibals!" she screamed. She stabbed a finger at the chief, who was looking at her in alarm. "So, that . . . that . . ." Grandma exploded, searching for the right word, "that good-for-nothing, pint-sized Romeo was only after my body!"

The chief backed slowly away from Grandma, as she lifted herself off the ground, her handbag gripped in her fist, and advanced toward him like an armored tank.

"Oh no," groaned Father, who had seen Grandma lose her temper before.

"Yikes!" whispered Morgan, who hadn't.

"What's wrong?" asked Mr. Bruce anxiously.

"What's wrong?" screeched Grandma, trying to get at the chief, who was hiding behind Mrs. Bruce. "I'll tell you what's wrong," she added fiercely. "That . . . that good-for-nothing, sweet-smiling, cheek-pinching, smooth-talking little dandy—" Grandma spluttered, forgetting, in fact, that the chief hadn't said a word to her—"has pulled the wool over my eyes. Blinded me with his charm, wormed his way into my affections." Grandma stopped for breath. "Deceived me," she said dramatically, "while all the time all he wanted to do was eat me!"

"There, there," said Mrs. Bruce soothingly, "he wouldn't mean any harm by it."

"It's just one of his funny little ways," added Mr. Bruce.

The chief peeped round at Grandma appealingly. "He probably thought you looked good enough to eat," Father suggested in a sugary voice, trying to calm Grandma down, as he didn't like the way some of the braver cannibals had picked up their spears again.

"Well!" said Grandma suspiciously, looking at the chief, who was studying his feet. "Well," she repeated doubtfully, as the chief peered shyly at her through his long lashes and risked a nervous little smile. "I suppose it could have been a misunderstanding," she added, looking into the chief's sad eyes. "But No Happen Again!" she said loudly, wagging her finger at him.

Father breathed a sigh of relief and Morgan looked at Grandma in awe. "I really thought she was going to bash him with her handbag," he whispered in admiration.

"Now then," said Mrs. Bruce cosily, when Grandma had calmed down and the chief came cautiously out from behind her skirt, "we've got so much to tell you we don't know where to begin."

"Well," said Father, eying the cannibals, "I think perhaps we'd all better go and tell Mother what's happened first. She'll be getting awfully worried."

Mrs. Bruce clapped her hands in delight. "Oh, how lovely!" she said. "Mother and the baby here as well. Oh, Robbie!" she added excitedly, "we haven't seen

Morgan's mother for over a year—and we haven't seen the baby at all. Imagine that! Nine months old he must be by now. Good heavens, how time flies! It only seems like yesterday when young Morgan was just a baby." She looked fondly at Morgan. "My, how he's shot up! And the spitting image of his father, isn't he, Robbie?" she asked. "Oh, we're going to have such a lovely chinwag," she continued, not waiting for Mr. Bruce's reply.

"Do you think," interrupted Father, "they would mind if we left now?" He nodded toward the cannibals.

"Of course not," laughed Mrs. Bruce, bending down to listen as the chief whispered something in her ear. "But the chief insists we all come back tonight for a feast."

"Oh!" said Grandma suspiciously, looking at the pot.

"I think we'd better be getting home," said Father quickly, and they all waved good-by to the chief and the rest of the cannibals, promising to return again that evening, and headed for home. Father strode ahead as quickly as he could, with Morgan trotting beside him to try and keep up, while Mr. and Mrs. Bruce ambled slowly behind, chattering sixty to the dozen to Grandma, who seemed to have completely forgiven the chief and was asking all sorts of questions about him.

Morgan was very thoughtful all the way home. "Why hadn't they eaten the Bruces?" he asked.

"I don't know," said Father. "I expect they'll tell us when we get home."

The Bruces' Story

"It was like this," said Mrs. Bruce, after they'd hugged Mother, played with the baby, and heard all about the family's adventures over a cup of tea. "We got onto the paddle steamer safely at Hull and were all having a really nice time, when suddenly the weather changed and turned a bit nasty. Well, we've seen storms in our time, haven't we, Robbie? But nothing like that one!"

Mr. Bruce nodded his head in agreement. "Aye!" he said. "That was a storm and a half, that one."

"Well," continued Mrs. Bruce, "we were blown completely off course, and instead of calling in at Robin Hood's Bay for a fish and chip supper, we ended up in the middle of the Pacific Ocean. Of course that upset some of the passengers, who demanded their money back, but as the captain said, it wasn't his fault and they'd have to take it up with Cook's when they got back. To make matters worse, we finished up stranded on a coral reef. It's a good job the captain managed to radio for help or I think he would have been thrown to the sharks by a rowdy group of ladies from Preston who threatened to sue him for loss of wages, as they should have been back at work six weeks before."

Mrs. Bruce stopped for breath.

"However," she continued, "he did manage to get everyone into lifeboats and as the paddle steamer was only half full, Robbie and I had a nice little one all to ourselves. We opened the bottle of wine Mrs. Goundry

kindly gave us—" she smiled at Grandma, who was beginning to wish she hadn't, as hers was empty now— "and very nice it was too," she added, "wasn't it, Robbie?"

"Aye!" said Mr. Bruce. "Very nice."

"By the time the helicopters had arrived to lift us off the boats," Mrs. Bruce went on, "we'd drunk all the wine, fallen asleep, and somehow drifted away from the paddle steamer. Still, the weather had improved by the time we were washed up on the island, so we didn't mind too much. As the bottle was empty, we thought it might be a good idea to put a message in it, like they do in the movies, and maybe someone would find it and come and rescue us."

"I found it! I found it!" Morgan interrupted excitedly. Mrs. Bruce smiled at him and patted his head.

"But how did you get to know the cannibals?" Father asked.

"And why didn't they eat you?" added Morgan.

"Ah!" Mrs. Bruce smiled. "I'm coming to that. Well, as I was saying, we were stranded on the island and decided to have a little stroll around to stretch our legs and perhaps see if anyone lived there."

"And then did you meet the cannibals?" asked Morgan.

"No, I'm afraid we did not!" said Mrs. Bruce grimly. "We were quietly strolling along, admiring the beautiful sunset, when we heard a funny scraping sound, as though someone was digging somewhere. Well! You can imagine how delighted we were to know that there was indeed someone else on the island, so we hurried over to where the noise was coming from, and in front of us we saw a group of men, spread out across the beach, carrying spades and obviously looking for some-

thing in the sand. The leader," Mrs. Bruce continued, "was rather a rough-looking gentleman who appeared to have a black patch over one eye."

"Yikes!" whispered Morgan, his face turning pink.

"However," said Mrs. Bruce, "we shouted greetings to them, but instead of returning them, they used some disgraceful language, waved their fists at us, and can you imagine," she added angrily, "started chasing us across the island, waving their spades at us! My blood boils when I think about it."

"And the cannibals?" Father interrupted.

"Ah yes!" Mrs. Bruce smiled again. "As I was saying, those unpleasant gentlemen chased us across the island and just as we thought they'd caught up with us, we happened to stumble over a group of charming little people who were bending down picking up coconuts that their comrades up in a tree had dropped down to them."

"The cannibals!" Morgan shouted.

Mrs. Bruce nodded. "Yes," she said. "And we were never more pleased to see anyone in our lives. When they saw who was chasing us, they appeared to lose their tempers and chased the ruffians back to the sea, throwing coconuts at them, with considerable force, I might add, for such small people. Robbie and I collected a pile of coconuts, which I carried in my skirt, and joined in the chase. The chief was delighted when Robbie bounced three in a row off the head of the leader of the gang, and cheered wildly every time he scored a direct hit. Unfortunately, they made their escape, but not before we'd bombarded their ship so badly it was letting in water by the time they managed to pull away from the beach."

"Aye!" said Mr. Bruce. "It can't have lasted long."

"Which it didn't, of course," said Father, "as they had to free the *Heart of Hull* from the coral reef to terrorize people in."

"I wonder what they were looking for on the beach," murmured Morgan.

"That I don't know," Mrs. Bruce admitted. "Robbie and I had a look, but we couldn't find anything. Anyway, you know what pirates are like, forever searching for buried treasure that doesn't exist half the time."

"Tell us about the cannibals," Father insisted.

"Oh yes!" said Mrs. Bruce, clapping her hands with delight. "Well, they seemed to take quite a fancy to Robbie and me for some reason and insisted on taking us back with them to their village."

"Didn't they want to eat you?" asked Morgan.

"Good heavens, no!" laughed Mrs. Bruce, waving her thin arms in the air. "Who'd want to eat a scraggy old beanpole like me? And as for Robbie here—" she chuckled, patting his bald head—"we reckoned that even marinated for a week he'd still be as tough as old shoe leather! Oh no!" she repeated. "They wouldn't want to eat us."

"They probably prefer someone with a bit more fat on them," said Father, all innocently, looking at Grandma, who ignored his remark and only sniffed.

"They sound awfully nice to me," said Mother, frowning at Father.

"Oh, they are!" said Mrs. Bruce. "Absolutely delightful! They wanted us to stay and live with them in their village, but we didn't want to intrude, so we built a nice little straw hut on the other side of the island, which the chief insisted on helping us with, and we pop in to see them quite often to say cooee."

"What does cooee mean?" asked Morgan curiously.

"It means 'hello' in cannibal language," said Mrs. Bruce.

Mr. Bruce looked at his pocket watch. "By gum!" he said. "It's half past eight already. The chief will be expecting us any minute."

"Do we have to go?" asked Father nervously.

"Yes!" said Mother, Morgan, and, surprisingly, Grandma.

"He'll be awfully upset if you don't," said Mrs. Bruce.

"That's true," admitted Father, thinking a happy cannibal chief is better than an upset one, and anyway, it did seem to be only Grandma he was interested in. So when Grandma had finished taking her curlers out and had sprayed herself with perfume, they put the baby in his stroller and set off back to the village.

There was really no need for Father to worry. The chief was very pleased to see them again, and as Mrs. Bruce said, any friend of theirs was a friend of the chief's, and he didn't eat friends. But Father was still a little bit wary, noticing the bones the chief wore around his neck, but Mrs. Bruce said that had happened a long time ago, and anyway the person it happened to was rather asking for trouble insisting that the cannibals wear proper clothes, and he was the only one who had any. Father had wondered where the chief had got his battered bowler hat.

The feast was really marvelous and lasted well into the night. The baby was made a great fuss of and handed round for everyone to admire, until he was so sleepy he was taken into a hut for a little nap.

Mother had a wonderful time, what with the huge orange moon and bright starry night and the gay music and mouth-watering food—it was just like the television advertisements for holidays in the tropics.

Grandma made a little bit of an exhibition of herself,

but as she was enjoying herself so much, no one seemed to mind. She flirted dreadfully with the chief, who flirted back of course, as he was very anxious to please her.

Morgan made lots of friends with the children of the village, although they couldn't understand each other, and had a grand time playing with the spears and bows and arrows that were stored in the chief's hut.

Mrs. Bruce, who had learned a little cannibal language, didn't stop talking all night, so she had a nice time, while Mr. Bruce puffed on his pipe contentedly, listening.

Even Father admitted it was a very nice evening and seemed a little disappointed when Mother said they really ought to get the children back home and into bed, and that Tailcat needed feeding anyway.

So once again they all said good-by to the chief, and thanked him for a lovely evening. Mother wanted the Bruces to come and stay with them, but they said it was an awfully kind offer, but they'd grown terribly fond of their little hut and if she didn't mind, they'd rather sleep there.

Grandma lingered a bit, not really wanting to go home, but when she saw that the chief was going to escort them part of the way, she didn't mind so much.

It was a warm, still night and the navy blue sky was sprinkled with millions of tiny stars as they strolled home, feeling very full and contented. When they parted company with the Bruces and the chief returned to his village, Mother sighed happily. "Wasn't it nice seeing the Bruces again?" she said.

"It certainly was," said Father, Grandma, and Morgan.

 *Buried Treasure*

Morgan woke up early the next morning. The sun was streaming through the gap in his bedroom curtains, and as everyone else was still asleep, he decided to go and play on the beach.

He took a spade from Father's work cupboard and crept quietly out of the house.

Father was in the middle of a lovely dream about steam engines, when suddenly a loud shout woke him up.

"What on earth is going on?" he cried, leaping out of bed and rushing to the door.

The shouting woke Grandma too, who had been asleep on the camp bed in the living room and was now complaining bitterly about all the noise, which of course woke the baby in the room above, who started rattling his cot to get out.

Grandma marched upstairs to Mother and Father's bedroom and hammered on the door.

"Good heavens!" gasped Father, opening the door and closing it quickly again.

"What's wrong?" asked Mother sleepily.

Father leaned weakly against the door, his face as white as sliced bread.

"There's a thing out there," he hissed, "with horrible spiky bits sticking up all over its head and a dreadful mask on its face! And it's trying to get in," he added in alarm, wedging his shoulder against the door.

"It's all right, dear," said Mother. "It's only Grandma with pipe cleaners in her hair and cold cream on her face."

"Are you sure?" asked Father, opening the door cautiously and peering at Grandma in disbelief. Grandma waved her arms angrily at him.

"When I went to bed last night," she said crossly, "I thought to myself how nice it will be to have a proper night's sleep for a change and not be thrown out of bed every time the house rolled." She patted the pipe cleaners in her hair.

"It's bad enough trying to sleep with these things sticking into your head all night," she added indignantly, "without having your beauty sleep disturbed at the crack of dawn by all that noise." She pointed downstairs just as the front door opened, and Morgan burst in.

"Quick, Dad," yelled Morgan, his voice hoarse from shouting, "come and see what I've found!"

Father sidled past Grandma, then raced down the stairs and disappeared after Morgan.

"Eeh, I don't know," Grandma muttered, fumbling her way back down to her bed. "Anyone would think we were stuck in the middle of Piccadilly Circus at rush hour instead of stranded on a desert island."

Mother decided she'd better get up and make the baby his breakfast, as he'd started hurling his teddy bears out of his cot and bouncing them against the wall and didn't seem to want to go back to sleep at all.

Grandma had just dozed off again, and Mother was tiptoeing past her bed on the way to the kitchen with the baby, when the door flew open and Father an Morgan stood in the doorway, their faces streaked with wet sand, as they staggered under the weight of a rusty old chest, which they carried between them.

"Quick!" shouted Father excitedly. "A screwdriver!"

"What's that?" asked Mother, looking at the chest curiously.

"Morgan found it," said Father. "It must be what One-Eyed Jake and his cronies were looking for."

"Do you think you ought to open it?" asked Mother doubtfully, handing Father a screwdriver.

"I wonder what's inside," whispered Morgan, gazing at the chest in awe.

"I don't know," murmured Father, "but I have a strange feeling I've seen this chest somewhere before."

Tailcat, who had noticed the baby safely out of grabbing distance on Mother's shoulder, crept warily into the room to have a sniff at the chest. Just as his nose touched the lock, it sprang open with a loud click. Tailcat leaped backward in surprise and landed on top of a gently snoring Grandma.

"Good heavens!" whispered Father, as he lifted the lid.

"Y-yikes!" stuttered Morgan, when he saw what was inside.

"Oh!" sighed Mother, her eyes shining. "How pretty!"

"What's happening? What's happening?" shrieked Grandma, sitting up jerkily like the Bride of Franken-

stein (as Father said later) and frightening the baby, who had wiggled out of Mother's arms and was trying to climb onto the bed after Tailcat.

Grandma stared in amazement at the glittering rubies, diamonds, emeralds, and pearls that cascaded out of the open chest.

"Morgan," said Father, pausing dramatically to pick up the screaming baby, *"has found the missing Crown Jewels!"*

"Eeh! Our Morgan!" Grandma whispered faintly. "Fancy that!"

10. The Trap

They all stared at the jewels in fascination. Grandma had a glazed look in her eyes as she clambered out of bed and walked slowly over to the chest, like someone in a trance.

"Eeh!" she repeated softly, fingering a diamond-encrusted crown with one hand and patting her curler-covered head with the other. "Do you think they would miss one tiny little crown?"

"Yes," said Father.

"Or maybe a teeny weeny one of these?" asked Grandma hopefully, holding up a tiara.

"Yes," said Morgan.

"Or even a very small necklace?" said Grandma wildly, "or ring? or brooch? I mean to say, they do belong to the Nation, don't they?"

Father shook his head.

Grandma sighed, thinking how much she would impress the chief if he saw her covered in jewels.

"Couldn't I even borrow something?" she said in desperation.

Father didn't like the way Grandma was eying the jewels and snapped the lid shut.

"Eeh!" said Grandma in alarm. "I felt right funny for a minute there, I can't think what came over me."

"Yoo-hoo! Can we come in?" a voice shouted from the doorway.

"How nice!" said Mother. "Mr. and Mrs. Bruce, won't they be surprised? Come in," she called. "Morgan's just found the Crown Jewels," she added proudly, as the Bruces strolled into the room.

"By gum," said Mr. Bruce, after he'd got over the shock of seeing Grandma in her curlers and the box of jewels on the floor. "Would you believe it, our Elsie?"

But for the first time in her life Mrs. Bruce was completely lost for words.

Then they all remembered. Of course, they'd seen the chest before. The newspapers and television had been full of it, showing pictures of the chest and offering huge rewards for its recovery, as it had been stolen over a year ago, when the Crown Jewels had been taken out for their annual cleaning and never been seen again.

Police all over the world had searched in vain, and although they suspected One-Eyed Jake had a hand in it, they'd never been able to catch him. There were rumors that Jake had been double-crossed by the cook, a nasty piece of work if ever there was one, and that he'd fled with the jewels and buried them somewhere. The cook, of course, had been thrown to the sharks when Jake found him, but Jake foolishly forgot to ask him where he'd buried the jewels until it was too late, and the cook was already disappearing into the mouth of a very hungry shark, who swallowed him in one gulp.

Since then Jake had sailed the seven seas searching for the treasure and attacking anything in sight as he was in such a bad temper about it all.

"One-Eyed Jake must have had wind that the treasure was buried here," said Mrs. Bruce, when she'd got her tongue back. "The chief told us they'd been here before making a dreadful nuisance of themselves until the cannibals had chased them off. Then lo and behold if they didn't turn up again the day Robbie and I arrived."

"Yes," Father agreed, "I think they must realize the treasure is on the island somewhere. And one thing is certain," he added. "They'll be back to look for it."

Grandma shuddered, then remembering the iron frying pan, went and brought it from the cupboard.

"Do you think they'll be awfully upset," said Mother anxiously, "when they discover that the treasure isn't buried anymore?" She frowned. "Of course, we could always tell them Morgan didn't find the treasure buried in the sand if they turn up, but that would be fibbing. Anyway," she added brightly, "as the treasure isn't buried anymore, they might not bother to come back and dig for it."

Father closed his eyes. "Don't you worry about it, dear. Morgan and I will think of something."

So while they thought, Mother made breakfast.

"Well," said Father, after they'd eaten their stewed bananas, "I think the only thing we can do is try to build a radio and call for help. A passing ship might pick up the message. We must get the jewels back as quickly as possible."

"But what about that cutthroat Jake?" Grandma demanded. "What if he gets here first? He's not likely to miss a three-storied house perched in the middle of the beach, now is he? And if he can't find the jewels, he's not going to be in a very good frame of mind."

"That's true," murmured Mr. Bruce, lighting his pipe.

"I don't think he'd attack during the day," said Mrs. Bruce. "He's too much of a coward for that, especially as we chased him off on his last visit." She shook her head violently. "Oh no! He'd probably come snooping about in the dark, when everyone is asleep."

"How thoughtless!" said Mother, freeing the cat's tail from the baby's fist. "Disturbing people's sleep like that."

Grandma shuddered again and gripped the iron pan tightly.

"I know!" shouted Morgan, who had been quietly. thinking. "Let's make a trap for them!"

"What a good idea!" said Mother.

"Marvelous!" said Father.

"What a clever lad," said Mr. and Mrs. Bruce.

"How?" asked Grandma, suspiciously.

"Dig a pit," said Morgan excitedly, "so they fall in!"

"But won't they see it?" asked Mother anxiously.

"Not when it's covered up," said Morgan.

"Oh!" said Mother. "But if they don't see the trap," she added thoughtfully, "how will they know where it is to fall in?"

"Come on, Dad," sighed Morgan, "we've work to do."

"Robbie and I will pop over and ask the chief to send some men to help," said Mrs. Bruce. "He'll be awfully upset if we don't."

Grandma's face lit up at the mention of the chief.

"I feel like a little stroll myself," she said. "I'll just

take my curlers out and dab a bit of lipstick on." She patted her head and giggled. "I don't want him to see me looking a mess," she finished, standing up and frightening the baby again, who had only just calmed down.

"There, there," said Mother, bouncing the screaming baby up and down. "It's only Grandma."

Grandma stumbled over the chest, and a funny look came into her eyes as she gazed at it.

"Don't wait for me," she said slowly to the Bruces. "I'll catch up with you later. That baby's tired out," she added to Mother, as the Bruces left. "I can tell by the way he's hollering."

"But he hasn't been awake very long," Mother protested.

"Then the poor little lamb wants his diaper changing," said Grandma firmly, guiding Mother to the bottom of the stairs.

"Don't forget to keep an eye on the jewels!" Father shouted, as he and Morgan hurried out of the house, carrying an extra spade.

"I won't," called Mother, as Grandma gently pushed her up the stairs.

"And wipe that sticky banana off his face and hands," Grandma added. "He looks as though he's been pulled through a hedge backward."

"But he always looks like that," said Mother, glancing at the baby in surprise. Grandma waited until Mother and the baby were safely upstairs, then she quickly dressed, pulled the curlers from her hair and a comb through it, dabbed some powder and lipstick on her face, and with a furtive look around, took a deep breath and very quietly opened the lid of the precious chest.

Mother was rather surprised, as she came back downstairs, to see Grandma stumbling out of the door with her overcoat wrapped tightly around her and spiky lumps sticking up from under her hat.

"Yoo-hoo, Grandma!" Mother called, as Grandma staggered across the hot sand. "You've forgotten to take your curlers out!"

But Grandma didn't answer. So, seeing the chest on the floor, Mother bent down to pick it up.

"Oh," said Mother happily, "I can lift it quite easily. I must be stronger than I thought." And humming softly to herself, she looked for a safe place to hide it.

11. Kidnapped!

It didn't take long to dig the pit, as the chief had sent over lots of men to help, and when the palm branches were laid across and sand scattered over it, it was impossible to tell where the beach ended and the trap began. Father sprinkled some small shells around the edge of the pit, so the cannibal children would know not to go near it, then he and Morgan went back to the house to search for bits to make a radio.

"Where's Grandma?" asked Father, as they entered the house.

"She went off to see the chief," said Mother.

"I thought it was quiet," murmured Father.

"That's odd," Morgan said. "We've just seen the chief. He came over with the Bruces to look at the trap, but Grandma wasn't with them."

"Oh dear," said Mother uneasily, "you don't think anything could have happened to her, do you? She did seem a bit strange earlier on."

"I shouldn't worry about that," said Father. "Grandma's always a bit strange. Perhaps she's got herself lost," he added hopefully.

"Well, I'm going to look for her," said Mother, putting the baby in his stroller. "I didn't like the way she looked this morning."

"Did anyone?" asked Father in surprise, as Mother went out of the door. "Anyway, I'm sure you'll find her, dear." Father sighed. "Grandma never seems to disappear for very long. By the way," he shouted after Mother, "where are the jewels?"

"I put them in a safe place," Mother shouted back.

"Oh dear," said Father, "Mother put the jewels in a safe place."

"Well," said Morgan, dismantling the baby alarm, "at least the pirates will never find them."

"That's true," murmured Father, "but will Mother? Good heavens!" he added suddenly. "How on earth did she manage to lift them?"

"Grandma must have helped," said Morgan. Father frowned.

"I suppose she must have," he said slowly.

Mother pushed the pram all around the island but didn't see any sign of Grandma. She stopped off at the Bruces' hut, but they hadn't seen her since breakfast either, so they all went to see the chief.

The chief seemed rather relieved that Grandma hadn't visited him, but being such a nice man, joined in the search, until it began to get dark, when they all decided they'd better go back to the house in case Grandma had found her way home again.

"Look!" whispered Mother, grabbing Mrs. Bruce's

arm, as they reached the house.
"Good gracious!" said
Mrs. Bruce. "Whatever next?"
Stuck in the door was
an evil-looking dagger, and
under the dagger, pinned to
the wood, was a grimy
piece of paper.

Mrs. Bruce pulled the dagger out of the door, just
as it flew open, and an excited Morgan hopped up and
down in front of them. A strange buzzing sound filled
the room as Morgan shouted, "We've done it! We've
done it!"

"Oh, the scoundrels!" exclaimed Mrs. Bruce angrily,
reading the note and passing it to Mother.

"It was all a bit faint," Morgan continued wildly,
"but someone answered our Mayday message!"

"Oh!" said Mother faintly, handing the paper to
Mr. Bruce.

Father appeared with a huge smile on his face, holding a strange contraption of knobs and wires above his

head. "On the baby alarm!" he added gleefully. "Aren't you pleased?" he asked, looking at Mother's glum face.

"Mrs. Goundry's been captured by pirates," said Mr. Bruce, handing the note to Father.

"Really?" said Father, eagerly taking the piece of paper. "Never mind, I'm sure they'll be only too pleased to give her back once they get to know her." His face fell as he read the note.

"What does it say? What does it say?" demanded Morgan, jumping up to try and read it.

Father handed the paper to Morgan. Written on it, and very badly spelled too, were the words:

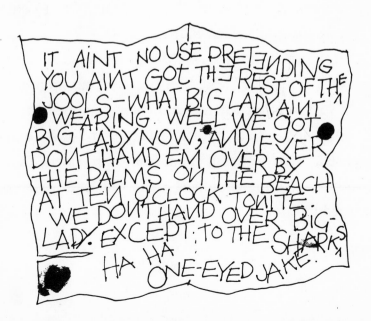

and written underneath, in Grandma's writing, was:

I only meant to borrow them

"Poor Grandma," Morgan whispered.

"Poor pirates," Father muttered.

"But what are we going to do?" wailed Mother.

"We'll just have to hand over the jewels to that terrible man," said Mrs. Bruce. "We can't allow Mrs. Goundry to be thrown to the sharks, can we now?"

"No," said Mother.

"No," agreed Mr. Bruce.

"No," said Morgan.

Father didn't say anything.

"We can't," wailed Mother, clutching her forehead.

"Can't what?" asked Father.

"Hand over the jewels," Mother moaned.

"Oh! Why not?" asked Father, perking up a bit.

"I've forgotten where I put them," sobbed Mother.

"Ah well," said Father, trying hard not to look pleased, "that settles it then. Still," he added, patting Mother's shaking shoulders, "she did lead a rich and rewarding life."

Mother sobbed even louder.

"At least we know the jewels are safe in the house somewhere," said Father. "Apart from the ones Grandma stole, of course."

"Borrowed," sniffed Mother.

"There, there, dear," said Father, handing Mother his handkerchief, "I'm sure Grandma would want to put the Nation above herself," he added, wincing. "The Supreme Sacrifice is but a small thing compared to the safety of our Nation's greatest heritage. Besides, she'll probably get a medal."

"Do you really think so?" said Mother, blowing her nose.

"Almost certainly," said Father. "Posthumously." He smiled gently at Mother. "In fact, you would probably be asked to collect it for her."

"Oh dear," sobbed Mother, "I don't think Grandma would like that. She's been trying for years to get invited to Buckingham Palace."

"She wouldn't know, dear, would she?" said Father kindly, making Mother burst into fresh floods of tears.

"Now don't you go getting yourself all upset," said Mrs. Bruce, patting an armchair for Mother to sit in. "It's only eight o'clock. That gives us another two hours to look for the jewels. Now you just put that baby to bed and sit yourself down quietly and have a little think while we search the house. Perhaps you'll remember where you put them if you have a little bit of peace and quiet."

"I don't think that will do much good," said Father cheerfully, as Mother took the baby upstairs. "The last time Mother put something in a safe place Morgan didn't get his Christmas present until the school summer holidays."

"Yes," sighed Morgan, "a bright red sled."

"Never mind," said Mrs. Bruce briskly. "The chief and I will search upstairs anyway. Robbie can look downstairs and Father and Morgan can do this room."

Father started looking halfheartedly under the carpet, while Morgan emptied every cupboard.

"It can't be under there, Dad," said Morgan. "You'd see the lump."

"Really?" said Father, smiling weakly and dropping the carpet back in place. "How silly of me. I don't know what I could have been thinking of."

"And it wouldn't fit behind a picture either," Morgan added, as Father lifted the painting of the *Flying Scotsman* off the wall and peered behind it. "There isn't room."

"I don't seem to be myself this evening," Father murmured, glancing at Mother, who had come back downstairs again and was talking to herself. "It's with worrying about Grandma, you know."

"First I took it upstairs," Mother was saying. "Then I decided it was better downstairs. Then I went upstairs again because the baby was crying. Then I decided to leave the baby until I'd hidden the chest because I couldn't carry them both. Then I sat down on the stairs for a while and thought. Then I came downstairs again and felt very hot . . ." Mother stopped suddenly and jumped up. "Hot!" she shouted.

Father and Morgan looked at her in alarm.

"Hot!" shouted Mother again. "Hot! hot! hot!"

"Yes, dear," said Father gently, "it's very hot. Now why don't you go to bed and have a nice little sleep? You'll feel much better in the morning."

"But it's not at all hot." Mother laughed, running across to the fireplace. "It hasn't been used since Christmas." And reaching up the chimney breast, she pulled down the sooty chest that was wedged there.

"Hooray!" shouted Morgan.

"Oh!" said Father gloomily.

"Have you found them?" shouted Mr. and Mrs. Bruce, running into the room with the puzzled chief behind them, who didn't know what he was supposed to look for, as Mrs. Bruce had forgotten to tell him.

"Well, thank goodness for that," sighed Mrs. Bruce. "Poor Mrs. Goundry will soon be out of the clutches of those dreadful men."

"And the jewels," said Father bitterly, "in them."

Morgan didn't say anything, but had the sort of look on his face he always had when he was thinking hard.

"The trap!" he shouted suddenly. "We'd forgotten about the trap! The trap is just by the cluster of palms where they want to swap Grandma for the jewels!"

"But how on earth will we lure them into it?" asked Father. "Now that they know we have the jewels, they'll be on their guard."

"We don't," shouted Morgan. "Don't you see? The trap is for Grandma!"

"Good heavens!" said Father slowly. "And once Grandma is safely out of the way . . . Chief," he said, "we're going to need your help again."

The chief beamed and nodded, as Mrs. Bruce bent toward his ear and translated Father's plan for him in cannibal language.

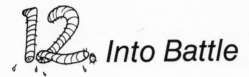 # Into Battle

There was so much to do before ten o'clock that Mother kept rushing around making herself and everyone else dizzy, until Father sent her up to the roof to keep an eye on the *Heart of Hull,* which he'd spotted through the binoculars anchored in the moonlit waters a short way from the beach.

Mr. and Mrs. Bruce asked for the old big pram (that Mother used only for shopping on Saturdays, as the baby always fell out of it), wheeled it quietly out of the house, and followed the chief back to the cannibal village with it.

Morgan fastened his snake belt around his waist and pushed his cricket bat through it, but as it kept tripping him up, he decided to carry it and put his slingshot there instead. Then he filled his pockets with marbles, put his space helmet on, and took the lid from a pan as a shield.

"Oh dear!" Mother's alarmed voice floated down the stairs. "They're climbing into the rowboat!"

Father looked at the clock. "I hope the chief gets back soon," he murmured, taking a big wooden mallet from his work cupboard.

"I can see Grandma!" Mother shrieked. "They're trying to lift her into the boat!"

"That should wear them out," said Father in satisfaction.

"Grandma's struggling," Mother continued anxiously. "It looks as if she has a bottle in her hand."

"Surprise, surprise," murmured Father.

"Oh dear," she added, "she's just broken it over Jake's head."

"It must have been an empty one," said Father.

"The boat's rocking!" cried Mother. "There's at least six of them trying to pull Grandma into it, no five— she's just knocked one into the water with her handbag. Oh, oh, there goes another one." Mother stopped for breath. "Oh," she said in disappointment, "she's in —but they're having to sit on her."

"Yikes!" whispered Morgan in admiration. "Wait till I tell them at school!"

"Cooee!" Mrs. Bruce's voice drifted in through the letter box. "We're ready."

"Right," said Father to Morgan. "Into battle!

"You stay here with the baby," Father shouted up the stairs to Mother, "where it's safe."

"No!" Mother shouted back, climbing down the ladder. "We're coming too!"

"Quick," said Father, pushing Morgan out the front door. "I'm afraid I'm going to have to lock Mother in." Then he raced upstairs, pulled the bolt on the landing door, and rushed out of the house.

The chief had brought all his men, some armed with spears and some with slings. The pram was piled high with coconuts, and it had taken both Mr. and Mrs. Bruce to push it as the load was so heavy.

Father looked at his watch. "Five to ten," he whispered. They could hear Grandma's muffled cries getting louder, as the pirates struggled across the water in the rowboat.

The chief and his men had already hollowed out places in the sand to hide, and at one minute to ten, Father, Morgan, and Mr. and Mrs. Bruce pushed the pram slowly across the sand and stopped a few yards away from the line of shells that surrounded the trap.

"Here they come!" hissed Morgan, as the pirates reached the beach and climbed out of the boat, half carrying a very angry Grandma. The pirates dragged Grandma toward the clump of palm trees, ducking every now and then as Grandma's arms flew out, grabbing at noses and ears and twisting anything she managed to get hold of, making the pirates howl in pain.

"I should think they'll be very pleased to get rid of her," Morgan whispered.

"Who wouldn't be?" murmured Father.

One-Eyed Jake squinted through the palms. "Is there anybody there?" he roared, being a bit shortsighted.

"Yes!" Father shouted back.

One-Eyed Jake heaved a sigh of relief.

"If you send Big Lady over," Father yelled, "we'll send over the jewels."

"Don't you Big Lady me!" Grandma's indignant voice snapped through the gloom. "I've had enough sauce from this side."

"We'll meet in the middle," growled One-Eyed Jake. "And no funny business," he added, pushing Grandma in front of him and waving his cutlass above her head, "or Big Lady in Big Trouble."

"Huh!" snorted Grandma, kicking Jake in the shins.

"Let me take the jewels," Morgan whispered.

"All right," replied Father, "but be careful."

Morgan took a deep breath and stepped slowly toward the pit, the box of jewels in his outstretched arms. One-eyed Jake seemed to be in quite a hurry to get rid of Grandma, who kept kicking him and complaining loudly about being pushed around as they advanced toward the other side of the trap.

"Right!" shouted Morgan, when his toes were touching the line of shells. "Let Grandma go, and I'll toss you the chest."

Then he hurled the jewels into the air, just as One-Eyed Jake gave Grandma a hefty push and cupped his hands to catch them. With a flash of pink bloomers Grandma disappeared head first into the trap after the chest.

"Aha!" screamed One-Eyed Jake in fury, when he realized where the jewels had gone. "So it's treachery now, is it? Come on, lads," he roared, glancing over his shoulder at his cronies cowering amongst the palm trees. "Come on," he snarled, "or I'll set about you myself, you mangy bunch of toothless yellow dogs!"

"Eeh," Mrs. Bruce breathed, "what a foul mouth that gentleman has!"

The pirates emerged reluctantly just as the chief signaled his men to attack.

Coconuts and spears whistled through the air, muskets boomed, knives flashed, cutlasses rattled, pirates shrieked, cannibals chanted, and sand flew everywhere!

"And now," screamed One-Eyed Jake, who was still facing Morgan across the pit, "to splice you into a million tiny pieces to feed my pet piranha!"

He leaped at Morgan, his cutlass flaying the air. Morgan ducked and held up his cricket bat. The cutlass sliced down to the handle, then stuck, quivering harmlessly in the bat, while One-Eyed Jake screeched in alarm as he felt the ground open under his feet, then somersaulted into the pit on top of Grandma.

"Take that!" Grandma's voice floated up from the

darkness. "And that! And that!" and after every "that!" there was a loud thump as Grandma set about Jake with her handbag.

"Look!" shouted Father, felling a pirate with his mallet. He pointed to the sea. Swimming furiously from the *Heart of Hull* and swarming onto the shore were more pirates. Dozens of them!

"Y-yikes!" stuttered Morgan, ducking again as a knife whistled past his space helmet.

Mrs. Bruce danced right up to the wet pirates, holding out her skirt, which was full of coconuts, with one hand, and bouncing them off the heads of the pirates with the other, skipping gaily in and out, dodging flaying swords with neat little sidesteps, tossing a coconut here and a coconut there, and dancing in circles around them, until they were quite dizzy and totally confused. Mr. Bruce galloped behind her, pushing the pram of ammunition, filling her skirt whenever it was empty, and stopping occasionally to take careful aim at any pirate Mrs. Bruce happened to have missed. But although Father and Morgan fought furiously and the

cannibals kept up a strong barrage of spears and coconuts and the Bruces' plan of attack was brilliant, there
were just too many pirates for them.

"It's no good," Father shouted to Morgan. "We're
not going to hold out much longer. We need help!"

"Yoo-hoo!" a cheerful voice sang through the noise
of battle.

"Good heavens!" said Father slowly.

Walking calmly toward them, with the baby in his
stroller, was Mother.

"I climbed out the window," Mother shouted proudly, "to give you a message."

"What message?" yelled Father, dodging a pirate that Morgan had felled with his slingshot.

Mother stopped in her tracks.

"Oh dear," she shouted, frowning to herself, "I've forgotten."

Father groaned. The pirates seemed to be winning now and had started rounding up little groups of cannibals.

"Oh!" Mother shouted in delight, pointing to the beach. "You can ask them yourself!"

Father looked toward the sea. Sitting majestically at anchor was an enormous liner. And jumping onto the beach from dozens of lifeboats were the passengers, crew, and captain of that liner—the *Queen Elizabeth II.*

"Hooray!" shouted Father, Morgan, Mr. and Mrs. Bruce, and the cannibals.

"Hooray! Hooray! Hooray!"

 **Rescued!**

When the battle-scarred pirates realized what was happening, they immediately surrendered. They'd had enough. Father and Morgan herded them all together and disarmed them. And what a sorry-looking bunch they were without their weapons.

The passengers from the *Q.E.2* were terribly disappointed at having missed all the fun and insisted that Morgan tell them all about it, blow for blow, while Father introduced the captain to everyone.

"Now," said Father, after everyone had been congratulated, "to retrieve the jewels."

He led the captain across to the pit. It was very quiet. The captain shone his flashlight into the darkness.

"Upon my soul!" he whispered, gazing at Grandma, who was busy trying on every piece of jewelry in the

chest with an unconscious One-Eyed Jake at her feet.

"Who," he asked, as Grandma smiled coyly at him, "is that ravishing creature?"

"Where?" asked Father, looking down, thinking perhaps he'd misheard and the captain had said ravaged.

"Such beauty," sighed the captain. "Such elegance and grace, such delicacy of movement."

Father peered about the hole again, but could see only Grandma and Jake. "You don't mean *him*, do you?" asked Father in horror.

Grandma fluttered her eyelashes at the captain. The captain clasped his hands together in delight. "My dear lady," he said softly, reaching his gloved hand down to Grandma, "allow me to introduce myself. Captain Stanley Cyril Rowbottom. Stan to my friends," he added, patting the diamond-encrusted hand she held up to him.

"Lily Victoria Goundry," said Grandma shyly. "Lil to my friends."

"Oh!" said the captain, clapping his hands together in ecstasy, "Lil. The most perfect of names"—he bent down again—"for the most perfect of women."

Grandma blushed. "Ta," she giggled.

Father looked in amazement at the captain. "Are you sure," he asked in astonishment, "that you're talking about Grandma?"

"If that glittering beauty down there is Grandma," said the captain recklessly, "then, yes!"

Good heavens, thought Father, the man's gone mad!

One-Eyed Jake opened his eye, saw Grandma, and jumped up in alarm.

"Get me out of here!" he shrieked. "Take me to prison, make me walk the plank, throw me to the sharks. Anything," he added desperately, "but please, please get me out of here!"

Grandma smiled sweetly at the captain, then delicately lifting up her bag, crashed it on Jake's head.

"Such fire!" breathed the captain in admiration.

"Help me! Help me!" Jake pleaded, throwing his arms up toward Father and making such a noise that everyone came running to see what was happening.

"Oh, the poor man!" said Mother, as Father and Morgan pulled him out of the pit. "I'll go and make him a nice cup of tea."

So while Mother went back to the house, the Bruces and the cannibals helped the captain get Grandma and the chest out of the pit. The passengers and officers returned to the *Q.E.2* with the handcuffed prisoners and Father and Morgan followed a meek One-Eyed Jake to where he'd hidden the jewels he'd taken off Grandma.

"Good heavens!" exclaimed Father, when he saw how many jewels there were. "Grandma took practically half of them!"

"That's why they were light enough for Mother to carry," said Morgan. "And to think we thought Grandma had helped to lift them!"

"Well," said Father, frowning, "I suppose she did lift them in a way."

They collected the jewels and returned to the captain, who was in deep conversation with Grandma (who seemed to have lost all interest in the chief— much to his relief), while the cannibals and the Bruces sipped cups of tea that Mother was handing round.

One-Eyed Jake turned very pale when he saw Grandma, and started shaking, but after Mother had made him sit down and drink a strong, sweet cup of tea laced with rum, he perked up a bit.

"Well," said the captain, gazing fondly at Grandma,

who had reluctantly put all the jewels back into the chest and was pouring a drop of rum into her tea to perk herself up as well, "we should all be grateful to this charming lady." He coughed gently. "Grandma to some," he said, smiling, "but Lil to her friends."

"Eeh, Stan," giggled Grandma, slapping his hand playfully.

"Who put all thoughts of personal safety aside," he continued, "to guard as many of the precious jewels as she could carry on her person. Knowing full well the terrible risks she might incur, undaunted she sailed through the challenge with great courage and spirit."

"The only spirit Grandma has in any great amount," Father whispered to Morgan, "comes in bottles."

"Ssh!" said Mother, as everyone clapped.

"And of course," the captain went on, as the applause faded, "none of that would have been possible if it wasn't for Morgan, who found the jewels in the first place."

Everyone cheered loudly, except for One-Eyed Jake, who scowled.

"And if Father and Mother and Mr. and Mrs. Bruce and the cannibals hadn't all helped," said Morgan shyly. Everyone cheered again.

"And I'm happy to say," said the captain, "that we sail at first light tomorrow, and you'll soon be back home again in England."

"But we don't have a home to go back to," said Mother forlornly, looking at the little house stranded in the middle of the beach.

"Never mind, dear," said Father, "maybe Charlie the builder will be able to build one just like it."

"It won't be the same, though," said Morgan sadly.

"Don't be too upset, dear," said Mrs. Bruce kindly, patting Mother's hand. "We'll keep an eye on it for you. It could always be your holiday home, you know."

"But aren't you coming back with us?" asked Father in surprise. Mrs. Bruce shook her head firmly.

"Robbie and I have decided to retire here and just potter about." She added, smiling at the chief, "The company is so nice."

"Well," said the captain, summoning the officers

who were waiting for him in a lifeboat, "I expect you'll
want to spend your last night here in your house, so
I shall wish you good night and send a boat over to
collect you at 6 A.M."

The officers picked up the Crown Jewels, handcuffed Jake, and led him away to the boat.

"Sweet dreams, Fair Lady," the Captain murmured,
kissing Grandma's hand. Then, with one last fond look
at her, he stepped into the boat too.

Mother wanted to go and say good-by to all the cannibals, so they went to the village, had a light supper
with the chief, and by the time they'd seen the Bruces
to their hut and returned to the house, it was quite late,
and they were all very, very tired.

A huge black cloud blotted out the moon as they opened the front door, and a sudden gust of wind rattled the open windows.

"It's raining," said Mother sadly, as they all took a long, last look at the house, "just like the day we sailed away."

"I wish we didn't have to leave the house behind," sighed Morgan.

"So do I," said Father.

Grandma was already fast asleep when Mother tiptoed past her to put the tired baby to bed.

And it rained so hard that night, and the thunder crashed so loudly, that no one heard Grandma complaining about a weazy stomach, or heard the thump as she was thrown out of bed.

# *All at Sea Again*

Father had set the alarm for five o'clock as they wanted to pack as many things as they could before the boat came to collect them. Mother shook Father and climbed sleepily out of bed when the alarm went off.

"Oh dear," said Mother, as she staggered across the room to draw the curtains. "My legs feel all wobbly."

"It's probably with upsetting yourself about the house," said Father, jumping out of bed and falling flat on his face.

"Look!" shrieked Mother, peering out the window through the gray light of dawn. "Oh, do come and look," she added, clapping her hands in delight.

Father crawled to the window, as he didn't seem to be able to stand, heaved himself up, and looked out.

"Good heavens!" he exclaimed, a slow smile spreading across his face. "Would you believe it?"

The door burst open and Morgan flung himself into the room. "Have you seen what's happening?" he shouted. "It's incredible!"

"Yes!" sighed Father and Mother, gazing dreamily into the water lapping gently around the basement windows, as the house drifted away from the beach.

"Will someone tell me what's going on?" demanded Grandma, staggering into the bedroom, clutching her stomach and looking very peaky.

"The house has decided to come with us," said Mother happily. "Isn't that lovely?"

"Oh look!" shouted Morgan. "The cannibals and the Bruces have come to see us off."

"How nice!" said Mother, going to get the baby and Tailcat.

They all hung out of the window, waving and shouting farewells, until the house had drifted alongside the *Q.E.2* and their friends were just tiny dots on the island.

"House starboard, sir," shouted a startled sailor, looking down at the sea. The captain peered over the side in amazement.

"Cooee!" giggled Grandma, who had braved the ladder (after having a drop or two of rum to settle her stomach), and was sitting happily on the roof with Father, Morgan, Mother, and the baby, having an early breakfast of fresh pineapple and coconut. The captain was quite overcome.

"My dear lady," he shouted down at Grandma, "destiny, knowing how every minute away from your radiant person seems like a hundred, has sent you to me before I even had time to man the boat to collect you."

"Oh," sighed Mother, "how romantic."

Yuk! thought Morgan.

"Actually," interrupted Father, "it was the storm."

"And we wondered if you would mind giving the house a lift home," added Mother, "if it's not too much trouble."

"No trouble at all," beamed the captain, "but first we must get you all safely on board." He summoned a sailor, spoke to him, then smiled gently at Grandma.

"Such a precious cargo," he added softly.

The smile Grandma returned to the captain froze on her face when she saw the cat's cradle the sailors were rigging up.

"Eeh!" she said in alarm. "I'm not getting into one of those things!"

"Come, come, delicate flower," said the captain coaxingly. "I assure you it is quite safe. Would I," he added, bending down to look into Grandma's eyes again, "entrust what I hold most dear to my heart to anything that wasn't?"

Father groaned. "Here he goes again," he whispered to Morgan.

"Trust in me, Sweet Lady," the captain continued, "and place your wonderful person in it."

"No!" said Grandma flatly.

"Then I," said the captain firmly, "shall bring you myself." And to everyone's astonishment, he leaped onto the rope, swung himself to the roof, grabbed Grandma around the middle, wedged her into the cat's cradle, then, sitting on top of her to stop her falling out, sailed across to the liner.

"Help!" shrieked Grandma, who couldn't see a thing as her hat had fallen over her eyes. "It's gone all dark!"

"Oh!" sighed Mother, as they collapsed on top of the sailors, who had been rooted to the spot in amazement. "Look at them! Just like Tarzan and Jane."

"Oh my!" Grandma giggled, catching her breath as the captain gallantly helped her to her feet. "You swept me right off my feet, you naughty man!" And while Grandma tottered off with the captain for a little glass of champagne to steady her nerves, Mother and the baby, Morgan and Tailcat, and finally Father landed safely on the liner, and smelling bacon and eggs, which

they hadn't had since the house sailed away, decided to go and have a second breakfast.

It didn't take long for the sailors to winch the house on board, in spite of the hundreds of passengers who thronged around, wildly excited about the whole thing.

"Oh dear!" said Mother, as they fought their way through the crowd to put the baby down for his morning nap. "I don't think he'll get much sleep with all this noise going on."

When eventually they reached the front door, their fingers ached from signing autographs and their jaws ached from smiling into cameras. Everyone wanted a conducted tour of the house of course, which made their legs ache as well, going up and down stairs all day long, and Mother was quite relieved when, after ten days at sea, the captain informed them they were due to arrive in Southampton the following morning.

"Oh good!" Mother sighed. "Miss Johnson will be pleased."

"Why?" asked Father in surprise.

"To get her end wall back, of course," said Mother.

15. Home, Sweet Home

"Oh, look!" said Mother, as they stood on the bridge with the captain. "It's just like Henley Regatta."

Bobbing up and down in the water were boats of all shapes and sizes, decorated in ribbons and flags and blowing their horns loudly as they escorted the *Q.E.2* toward Southampton Docks.

"Good heavens!" said Father, as the liner approached the shore. "Look at all those people!"

The docks were jam-packed with jostling crowds, waving Union Jacks and shouting and cheering at the top of their voices.

"Look!" shouted Morgan. "I can see the Prime Minister over there!"

"And television cameras!" screamed Grandma, gulping down the drink the captain had poured her and rushing off to the ladies' room to powder her nose.

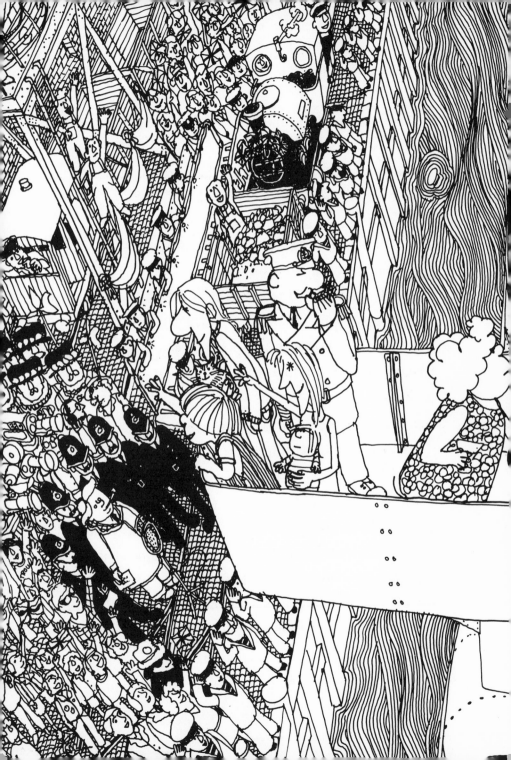

"Sweet impetuous maiden," sighed the captain, blowing a kiss after her.

The noise was deafening as the pilot boat guided the liner toward the edge of the dock.

"Yoo-hoo, Morgan!" shouted a group of children, waving a huge photograph of Morgan above their heads.

"My class!" shouted Morgan in delight, as he recognized his friends.

"How nice," said Mother, as Morgan waved to them. "They must have been given the day off from school to come and meet you."

"It's Saturday," Father murmured.

"Really!" said Mother in surprise. "I thought it was Sunday."

"Eeh!" puffed Grandma, reappearing through a cloud of face powder. "I feel all hot and bothered."

"My dearest Lil," said the captain, gazing at Grandma adoringly, "you look divine. As always."

"He can't have seen her in her curlers yet," Father muttered.

"Ta," giggled Grandma, patting her hair. " I didn't want to look a mess in front of all those television cameras."

"And now, my sweet lady," said the captain, "Morgan and I must go and collect the precious Crown Jewels. As he found them—" he smiled—"he must have the privilege of returning them to the Prime Minister." He patted Grandma's hand, spilling some of the drink Grandma was pouring into her empty glass. "The glittering Crown Jewels," he added softly, "outshone only by your beauty."

"And her nose," Father murmured.

The crowd were beside themselves with excitement as the gangplank was lowered and twenty smart sailors in dress uniform formed a guard of honor for Morgan and the captain, who were carrying the chest of jewels on a silk cushion, Father and Mother, who were carrying the baby and Tailcat, and Grandma, who was carrying a half-finished glass of champagne.

Everyone cheered as the Prime Minister stepped forward to greet them, and Morgan (helped by the cap-

tain as the chest was so heavy) handed him the Crown Jewels. The Prime Minister took the chest, staggered, and quickly gave it to several strong Beefeaters, who were standing next to him, to put in the armored truck that was parked nearby. Then he held his hand up for silence and produced a letter from his pocket.

"I have here a letter," the Prime Minister said into the microphone.

"We can see that," a voice shouted from the crowd. "Get on with it."

"A very special letter," the Prime Minister continued, ignoring the heckler, "for a very special person. And from a very special person.

"This letter," he went on, waving it above his head, "is from Her Majesty the Queen."

"Hooray!" everyone cheered.

"And," said the Prime Minister, "it's addressed to Morgan."

The crowd cheered again.

"Oh!" whispered Mother, nudging Father, "the poor things couldn't afford a stamp."

"Which I shall read to you," continued the Prime Minister, smiling at Morgan. "If Morgan doesn't mind, of course." Morgan shook his head.

"It says—" the Prime Minister put on his glasses and looked at the piece of paper—" 'Buckingham Palace, June 4th. My husband and I, and all the members of the Royal family, send our heartfelt thanks and warmest congratulations to our loyal subject, Morgan, for the finding and recovering of our country's most valued inheritance, the Crown Jewels. We regret not being able to meet him on his return due to an indisposition of flu, but invite him, and his family, to tea on Sunday, when we very much hope they will accept a medal as well as the reward. Her Majesty, The Queen.' "

The crowd cheered wildly and stamped their feet and threw their hats high into the air with delight.

"Do you think Princess Anne will be there?" Morgan whispered, as the captain revived Grandma with a sip of champagne.

The Prime Minister held his hand up for silence again. " 'P.S.,' " he added. " 'The Princess Anne will be looking forward to meeting them.' And now," he shouted above the clapping, "I propose three cheers for Morgan. Hip-hip!"

"Hooray!" the crowd shouted.

"Hip-hip!"

"Hooray!!" the crowd screamed.

"Hip-hip!"

"HOORAY!!!" everyone roared.

And while Father, Mother, Grandma, and Morgan signed autographs, shook hands with everyone, and were interviewed for television and the newspapers, the house was transferred to a tug, taken along the Thames, put onto a truck, and cemented back into its foundations by Charlie the builder.

"Well," said Mother, as they walked up the garden path later that day, "what a lot of excitement!"

"Yes," said Father, "and tomorrow we'll see the Queen."

"And collect the reward," Morgan added.

"And I," giggled Grandma, "will be getting engaged."

"What!" said Father.

"The captain asked me to marry him," said Grandma.

"Good heavens!" said Father.

"How nice!" said Mother.

"Still," Father murmured, as they opened the front door, "I suppose that will mean you'll spend a lot of time at sea."

Then they all felt so tired they went straight to bed.

"I'm so glad," said Mother, as she put out the light, "that Grandma didn't have to collect her medal posthumously."

"Are you, dear?" asked Father, and fell asleep.